MOONFIXER

APPALACHIAN JOURNEY

BOOK 2

CC TILLERY

Spring Creek Press

Copyright © 2013 CC Tillery

First Edition

ISBN 0989464121:
ISBN-13: 978-0-9894641-2-3

Published by
Spring Creek Press
Hendersonville, NC

Dedication

To our father, Raymond Earl "John" Tillery, for your constant encouragement and unending support as well as all the wonderful stories you told us over the years about Bessie and her family. We love you very much, Daddy!

To our uncle, Ken Elliott, for sharing anecdotes about growing up on the mountain which brought the mountain people so vividly to life and for your generosity in allowing us to pen some of those stories here. We send our love.

And, of course, to our great-aunt Bessie Daniels Elliott and great-uncle Fletcher Elliott for sharing this journey with us in spirit. We can only hope we're doing your story justice!

CHAPTER ONE

Summer 1906

They ain't been married long enough to wrinkle the sheets.

I first heard the ghosts on a midsummer night in 1906. No more than a whisper of sound, it was enough to make me sit up and crumple the shirt I was mending in my hands. The old hound dog napping at my husband's feet startled awake and let out a soft whine. When I looked down at him, his eyes were fixed on the darkness outside.

I jumped up, the shirt dropping to the floor, and rushed over to the open window as the whisper turned into a more audible shuffle followed by a thump as if someone were dragging a heavy chest through the possum trot that ran between our house and the old shack next door.

The breeze picked up, the scent of cedar mixed with pine spicing the air as the katydids, crickets and frogs abruptly ended their contest to see which could vocalize the loudest. Placing my hands on the windowsill, I leaned out and shivered in the air that felt more like winter than summer.

I stared into the night hoping to see...something. I wasn't sure what, some nocturnal creature hunting for food, an unexpected visitor stopping by for a quick cup of coffee before he continued his journey home, or perhaps one of the chickens in a mad escape from the coop, celebrating its freedom.

Nothing but the blackness of night lit only by the sliver of a waning moon riding low in the sky.

Fritz, the stray hound dog who had followed Fletch home one day shortly after we took up residence in the house, came up beside me and leaned against my leg. I scratched behind his ear and he cocked his head in the manner of dogs everywhere when they're puzzled.

As mystified as the dog, I tilted my own head, unsure what I was hearing.

A mellifluous murmur joined in the shuffling and I jerked my eyes back to the window. "Swing low, sweet chariot," followed by a melodious answering of several male voices, "Comin' for to carry me home."

My fingers gripped the windowsill and, without thought, my lips moved as I silently voiced the next words with that honeyed solo voice, "I looked over Jordan and what did I see?" and the harmonious response from the others, "Comin' for to carry me home."

Bending forward, I held my breath as a new sound joined the singing. I didn't know what it was at first and squeezed my eyes shut, trying to picture what would make that somehow worrisome jangling noise. The image came to me as clear as day: chains, the clanking of shackles around the ankles of slaves, their bare feet shuffling in a double line through the possum trot outside our house.

I'd never heard the sound before but knew without a doubt what it was.

I stared at the blankness outside the window. If I could hear them, I should be able to see them, shouldn't I, I thought as those melodious voices continued.

"A band of angels comin' after me, comin' for to carry me home." And then all joined together in the chorus, "Swing low, sweet chariot, comin' for to carry me home, swing low, sweet chariot, comin' for to carry me home."

In my mind, I pictured a double line of Negroes dressed in ragged pants, most with equally tattered shirts on their backs, but a couple shirtless, all barefoot, all seemingly healthy except for one dragging a mangled leg behind him. That was where the thump came in; he would draw the wounded leg forward, brace himself for a fleeting moment on the injured foot then bring the other one forward quickly, planting it with a thud in the dirt before starting the whole process over again.

It was painful to envision. Though I couldn't literally see them, I could hear them, and my imagination took care of the rest.

The voices grew fainter as they moved on to the second verse and I stood frozen for a few moments, straining to hear every word while continuing to stare into the darkness. When their voices faded to a barely heard murmur on the night air, I leaned out farther, once more hoping to catch a glimpse of...I didn't know exactly what. A gleaming of dark skin in the moonlight, a stirring of the dirt as the last of them moved beyond the possum trot, a shivering of the leaves on the hollyhocks thriving in the little flower garden at the corner of the house; some movement to mark their passing. But there was nothing, only the faint echo in my head of the old Negro spiritual accompanied by the ominous clanking and the shuffle thud of bare feet.

I stayed there for several minutes, still hoping to see what I could so clearly picture in my mind. When the crickets started up again, joined by the katydids and frogs, I gave up and went back to my chair.

It seemed the gift I inherited from my Cherokee ancestors had not, as I thought, left me when I married and traveled over the mountains with my new husband to live in the Broad River Township of North Carolina.

I could count on the fingers of one hand the number of times it had appeared before my marriage but there had been a definite absence since that train trip. The only indication- the gift was still with me occurred when Fletch took me to meet Mr. and Mrs. Solomon in hopes of talking the old man into selling us a parcel of land we could farm and make our home.

The Zachariah Solomon Plantation sprawled over one side of Stone Mountain and had been in the Solomon family for years. The owner at that time, Mr. Edwin Solomon, was a hale and hearty man in his early seventies when we'd visited with him and his wife on the front porch of their home. After several minutes, he took me by the arm and led me over to his frog pond, a wide dip he'd carved out of the dirt and lined with rock. According to Mrs. Solomon, he loved that pond more than he loved her.

As I looked down into that slightly murky water, watching the frogs swim or laze on the rocks piled at the edge, Mr. Solomon said, "Needs to be cleaned but it gives me what I want." He'd winked and gone on, "Fresh frog legs ever once in a while. Ever had frog legs, Missus Bessie?"

I went still, frozen with the thought that flashed through my mind: *Be careful when you clean it, Mr. Solomon, or it will give you something you don't want.*

The warning disappeared as quickly as it surfaced, and though I felt I should tell him, I resisted for fear he would think me strange and might even refuse to sell us the land when Fletcher approached him.

I've often wondered if things would have turned out different if I had said something. But I kept my silence and less than a year later, Mr. Solomon had cleaned his frog pond, paying no attention to the open cut on his hand. A few days after that, the cut became infected. A stubborn old cuss to the very end, he refused to make the trip to Old Fort to have the sole doctor in town treat him. Mrs. Solomon, as most mountain women did at that time, took matters into her own hands, attempting to cure the infection herself with a variety of herb and plant tinctures and salves, but nothing worked. A few short weeks later, Mr. Solomon died from blood poisoning.

Could I have prevented this if I had overridden my qualms about the way people might see me if they knew I sometimes had feelings about things that hadn't happened yet? I had no way of knowing, of course, but worried about it nonetheless.

Most troublesome to me was the thought that Fletcher and I had indirectly profited from the old man's death. If he had lived, would he have given in and sold us the property, after all?

Most likely not. He'd been a might obstinate about keeping the old plantation intact and had flat out refused to sell when Fletcher approached him about it, saying he didn't feel right selling off what his great-great-grandfather Zachariah had built from scratch.

When her husband died, Mrs. Solomon didn't have any interest in holding on to the family legacy and neither did her son, a lawyer who had moved to Savannah to escape the snowy winters in the North Carolina Mountains. Almost as soon as they buried their patriarch, Randall Solomon put out the word that the old Zachariah Solomon plantation was to be sold. Fletcher and I had been among the first buyers, purchasing 400 acres of beautiful, mostly untouched mountain land.

The first time Fletch brought me to see this place, this house with the run-down shack beside it, a possum trot running between them, and the old slave cabins near the trickling creek flowing through the front yard, a sense of rightness came over me, a welcoming of sorts that I hadn't felt before. This then, I thought, this tiny cabin was where Fletcher and I were meant to spend our life together. I had found my place in the world.

But the finding had come at a price: a death I possibly could have prevented if only I'd had the courage to speak up.

Shaking off the gruesome thought, I pondered why the gift had decided to come back after such a long time. Fletcher and I had lived with his family on this same mountain for the first five years of our marriage, and other than the time with Mr. Solomon, I hadn't felt so much as a stirring in my mind. And even then, it had been no more than a glimmer that fled almost before I could get a grasp on it.

Could it be the house? Was it possible the location had whispered to me the first time I'd seen it? Had it drawn me in with that strange yet oddly familiar feeling of homecoming? Were the ghosts speaking to me even then?

I was 25 years old and had been teaching for five years. Although Fletcher and I had been married just as long, we had not yet conceived a child—something I was torn about—and I wondered if, despite the Queen Anne's Lace seeds I chewed every morning, I had somehow managed to conceive. A woman's body went through many changes when she was with child. Could that be it?

Instinctively, I shied away from that. I did not want to have children yet. I was not ready for the changes motherhood would bring about.

I wished for someone to talk to, but since Fletch and I came to the mountain, the only person I was really close to was Fletcher's mother. I shook my head at that. Ma Elliott was kind and wise to a certain extent but I had no idea how she would react if I told her about hearing ghosts outside my window.

The mountain people, while friendly and gracious, were a superstitious lot, living their lives by an old and unspoken code. There was a reason for everything, and if there wasn't, well, then look to God and mayhap you'd find the explanation. God, they often said, worked in mysterious ways and it wasn't for them to question His dealings but to accept and go on with the life He'd given them.

As a precaution against the whims of God, they followed the moon almost as religiously as they did the holy Bible. The lunar phases dictated a good deal of what they could and couldn't do: plant during a full moon if you wanted a bountiful harvest unless, of course, you were planting root crops and then you should plant during a waning moon; never gather your crops during a black moon, only during the full moon if possible; and always, always, wait for a full moon before you visited the doctor, no matter how sick you were. They even married by the moon.

A way of life, I often thought, similar to my ancestors, the Cherokee. My great-grandmother Elisi would certainly understand and most likely approve.

Fritz heaved a world-weary sigh as he settled in again at Fletcher's feet, shut his eyes and promptly fell into another nap.

Outside, a sudden gust of wind rustled the leaves of the hollyhocks and the curtains billowed out from the window. I could smell rain on the air and it was like an answer to my prayers. I knew what I should do. I couldn't talk to anybody on the mountain about this, so I would talk to Elisi. Since she was miles away, I would write her a letter.

Elisi had taught me much about my somewhat ethereal feelings during the time she stayed with us after we lost my little brother Green to a flash flood in the spring of 1899. It was a horrible time for my family, made all the worse because we lost Mama to milk fever following the birth of my little sister Frances Ann, or Jack as Papa called her, in December of that same year. I turned 18 shortly after Mama died, and while I was still a child in most people's eyes, Death forced me into growing up. And when I found a sick Melungeon girl hiding in the hayloft of our barn and tried to save her, she'd died, too, at the hands of a drunken doctor whom Papa had trusted to do an operation which I knew would kill her.

For a time, it seemed as if Death had taken up permanent residency in my life. I errantly blamed Papa for Druanna's death, refusing to see that he was doing the only thing he knew to do to try to save her. Papa and I were at odds for the longest time after that but had been slowly inching our way back together when I chose Fletcher Elliott to give me a kiss after finding the red ear of corn at Mr. Dunlap's annual corn shucking. And when Fletcher proposed after Aunt Belle's Breaking Up Christmas party and I'd accepted, Papa had withdrawn again.

If it hadn't been for Elisi, I don't think I could have survived that time of unutterable grief followed by the alienation of my father, the man I'd always adored and admired beyond anyone else.

Elisi, with her little bits of wisdom and her knowledge of Cherokee medicine, had seen the woman I wanted to be and sagely guided me through a time when I questioned even my own judgment. She encouraged me to live the life I wanted instead of looking to the acceptable etiquette of the time and allowing it to mold me into someone I could not respect, much less try to emulate.

It was Elisi who showed me what it was to be a whistling woman, something I was still striving to do after five years of marriage. And it was Elisi who told me I would come through with the help of one person, and though she hadn't identified the person, I knew without a single doubt it was the man I married.

And it was Elisi who taught me to smell the rain.

The memory of that warmed me and I made up my mind to write her. I wished I could talk to her right then, but while the world was a quickly changing place in 1906, with the new-fangled contraption called a telephone in the bigger cities, that convenience, if it could be considered such, had not yet made it to the mountains. Since talking to her was not to be, I'd have to be patient and wait for the whims of the United States Postal Service.

Of course, I could always talk to my husband. Fletcher, a naturally quiet soul, was a good listener, but while we could no longer be considered newlyweds, as Elisi would say, we hadn't been married long enough to wrinkle the sheets on our marriage bed.

Fletcher snorted awake beside me. I looked over at him as he stood up, stretched his arms over his head and then ran his hand over his face. I could hear his calloused fingers as they rasped over his stubbled jaw.

Outside, the singing started up again, fainter now as if coming from inside the slave cabins. I'd never heard this song, something about Balm of Gilead. Elisi had collected Balm of Gilead buds and made a salve to treat various skin ailments or a liniment for sore muscles but I didn't think this song was about the plant. More likely it referred to the Balm of Gilead mentioned in both the Old Testament and New Testament of the Bible.

I jumped up and ran over to the window. With my back to him, I said, "Fletcher, do you hear that?"

I looked over my shoulder and saw him cock his head to the side. It seemed everyone in our little family was puzzled tonight. Sitting back down, he shrugged. "Hear what?"

The singing continued but the clanking of ankle chains was absent as was the sound of bare feet shuffling over hard-packed earth. I leaned out the window, looking toward the small shacks.

"Hear what, Bess?" Fletcher repeated.

"Come over here and see if you can hear it."

I bit my lip, trying to decide how best to explain to him that I had heard a group of slaves walking by our open window, singing a gospel song to the accompaniment of chains around their ankles.

He came up beside me and put his arm around my shoulders, listening intently for a moment as he leaned out the window. After several seconds, he said, "I don't hear anything, Bess, except the crickets and that old bullfrog down to the creek. Want me to go out and check?"

I shook my head as the singing faded away completely. "Must've been some night creature outside looking for food. It's gone now."

"I'll go out and check if you're scared, Bessie."

"No, it didn't scare me. I only wondered what it was. I don't hear it anymore. Whatever it was, it's gone and won't bother us again."

He dropped his arm and turned to face me, taking my hand. "What is it, Bessie?"

I sighed. Fletcher sometimes knew me better than I knew myself. It was eerie enough at times to make me think I wasn't the only one in this marriage who had a gift.

I took it as a sign that the time to speak to him about my somewhat ambiguous ability was nigh. "Zachariah Solomon used to have slaves, didn't he?"

"Yep, back before the war. Not very many but he had some."

"Field workers?"

He shrugged. "I guess but he probably had some house servants, too."

I hoped he could handle the fact that his wife sometimes knew things before they actually happened and now, apparently, could also hear ghosts. "I just heard a group of slaves outside the window. They were shackled." I shivered, thinking of how they must have been treated but shook it off. That was in the past, thank goodness, and fretting about it now wouldn't make it any easier on them. "And they were singing as they moved through the possum trot."

Fletch considered this for what seemed a lifetime but I imagine was only a few seconds. "What were they singing?"

9

"Swing Low, Sweet Chariot and then another song I've never heard, something about the Balm of Gilead, but they started with *Swing Low, Sweet Chariot.*"

He smiled. "I'd like to have heard that. It's one of my favorites."

I merely stared at him, my mouth hanging open which made him laugh.

"This was the overseer's house, you know, Bessie, so I guess it's natural to have the slaves parading by for some sort of inspection or something." He shook his head. "Or maybe they had to pass this way to get from the fields to their quarters. Don't really know how it all worked and I'm glad not to be a part of it but I'd say the slaves were all over this part of Zachariah's land what with those shacks being their homes and the overseer living right here." He squeezed my hand and yawned. "We better get ourselves off to bed, Bessie girl. Folks're bound to start arriving early in the morning to help with the barn."

I nodded. Tomorrow was to be our barn-raising, or whatever you called it when neighbors gathered to help repair an old barn. There would be no "raising" since the barn was already built, but there would be quite a bit of repairing and rebuilding.

I went back to my chair, picked up the shirt, folded it and tucked it into my mending basket sitting on the floor. I hadn't made much progress on it that night but then I'd never been much with a needle and thread, not like Mama or my sister Loney, who both stitched beautifully. Any excuse for me to put needlework aside to be done later was welcome.

As I followed Fletcher to our bedroom, I marveled at his quiet acceptance of my unusual story of hearing ghosts. I often thought there was nothing I didn't know about my husband, it seemed I still had a lot to learn about this quiet, gentle, stalwart man I loved.

I changed into my nightgown while Fletcher made a quick trip to the outhouse. I climbed into bed and watched Fritz amble in and curl up in his customary spot on the floor in front of the chest in the corner. As I waited for Fletcher to come back and douse the kerosene lamp, I wondered if I would dream of wandering spirits that night or if I would be able to fall asleep at all. It seemed to me my natural curiosity and inquisitiveness about what had just happened would most likely keep me from a peaceful slumber.

While I didn't dream about them that night, I would hear the slave ghosts numerous times over the many years Fletcher and I lived in that house. I never actually saw them, which I suppose is something to be grateful for, but I heard them singing and shuffling along the possum trot even when it wasn't a possum trot anymore. Some years later, Fletcher tore down the shabby little house next to us and the passageway became no more than a worn path beside our house where I tried several times to plant flowers and other plants but nothing ever took hold in that narrow strip of earth. I eventually stopped trying, ceding the path to those bare ghost feet of the singing slaves I never did actually see.

But I heard them. And I would hear others before it was all said and done.

CHAPTER TWO

Summer 1906

Those young'uns could worry the dead.

The next morning we had a crowd of people who did, indeed, show up early as Fletcher had predicted. The men folk came armed with hammers and saws and other tools they would need throughout the day and the womenfolk brought baskets packed full of food. Our front yard teemed with children laughing and playing games of tag and hopscotch in the squares they'd drawn in the dirt. I worried at first about them playing so near the creek and pointed it out to several of the women but they waved my concerns away.

Sarey Henson flicked her hand in dismissal. "Law, Bessie, them little-uns learned to swim practically afore they learned to walk. They're like fish now and, 'sides, the older ones have been charged with keeping their eyes on the younger ones. They'll not let anything happen to them young'uns."

I had no option but to be satisfied with that so went around back to check on the food. The tables were laden down with enough to feed two armies. The women had outdone themselves, bringing baked hams, fried chicken, fresh green beans, early squash, biscuits, honey, apple butter and various types of sweets; apple stack cake, spice cakes and bread pudding.

The men all seemed happy to work side by side to build Fletcher's "fancy barn" as they called it. Knowing my love for the old cantilevered barn out behind our house in Hot Springs, Fletcher had drawn up plans to convert the decidedly plain barn to a cantilevered one. I couldn't imagine how it could be done but Fletch was almost as good a builder as Papa. Of course, Papa had more experience and usually built from the ground up but Fletch was pretty sure his plans would work.

Right about noon, I walked up to the back porch and pulled on the old cow bell Fletch had hung outside the door. Almost as one, the men put down their tools and scrambled down the ladders or out of the barn to the horse trough to wash up. It was customary for the men folk to be served first. After that, the women would tend to the little ones and finally fill their own plates. I had no children to see to, so after we all joined hands and Fletcher said grace, I filled a plate for him then helped the mamas who had more than a few young'uns to see about, which was, in truth, most of the women. It seemed to me that the only value placed on womenfolk at that time was how many children they could turn out in the course of a few years. Which was only fitting, I suppose, since the children, when they grew, would be put to work on the farm, in the livery, cutting trees, or whatever else the father did to support the family.

With their bellies full, the men went right back to work while the women covered up the food left on the tables, chatting about which dish was the most popular, exchanging recipes and cooking tips. I listened avidly, hoping to catch some insight into preparing the different meats Fletcher sometimes brought home from hunting. Squirrel, possum, rattlesnake, and bear, they were all foreign to me and I often found myself stumped on the best way to cook them.

Fletcher could usually tell me but since I trusted the women's recipes more than his sometimes offhand, "Just throw it in a pot and boil it with some taters," I paid close attention to what they had to say.

Olivia Cross was in the middle of telling me her recipe for squirrel and possum stew when one of the children screamed in the front yard.

The sound sent chills up my spine and I froze for a few

seconds. When the other children didn't start laughing, all I could think about was what had happened when Green died, that high-pitched squeal followed by Loney and Roy yelling. I swan, my heart stopped completely and then, with a painful thump, started back up at a furious pace.

A high-pitched screech finally registered and I dropped the bowl of corn I was holding. It shattered at my feet, sending shards of china and the remaining kernels of corn spewing up in a rainbow that splashed mine and Olivia's skirts.

"Law, what in the world?" Olivia asked as she turned around to look for the source of the scream.

I knew but didn't answer, just turned and started running around the side of the house, grabbing the old hoe I kept beside the back door as I went. Ever since I came upon a rattlesnake sunning itself outside the barn, that old hoe had become my constant companion whenever I walked out the door. Fletcher sometimes teased me about it but I was dreadfully scared of snakes and wasn't going to take a chance on meeting up with another one without a weapon in hand.

In the front yard, the children were gathered around in a circle, strangely silent now except for a couple of the younger girls who were crying, little Gerald Davis sprawled on the ground at their feet. Two of the boys broke away and went running toward the barn, calling for their fathers.

I skidded to a halt beside Gerald then went down on my knees. His face paper white, he held his left leg up in the air. I could see the two holes in his trousers right below the knee and turned around to snap at the girls, "One of you go get me a knife. Another of you go tell someone to start a pot of coffee and tell them to make it strong."

No one moved until I clapped my hands together and yelled, "Now!"

Some of the men had reached us by then and Gerald's father knelt down on the other side of him, placing his hand on the boy's shoulder. His mother came up next, her eyes like saucers in her pale face. She looked at me, took a deep breath, then laid her hand on her husband's arm to get his attention and stop his frantic patting of Gerald's chest. "Move back, Vern, and let Miss Bessie work," she said in a low voice.

Fletcher appeared beside me, a jug of moonshine in one hand and a knife in the other. "She knows what she's doing, Vern. Let her help your son." He handed me the knife. "It's clean, Bessie. I poured some of Pa's moonshine over it."

I looked at him and, like Mrs. Davis, took a deep breath before speaking. "Can you tear his pants leg so I can get a closer look?"

He bent down and without further ado ripped the seam of the pants until they gaped open to little Gerald's bony knee.

Pulling my handkerchief out of my sleeve, I quickly tied it around Gerald's leg, just above where the snake had bitten him. Next, I examined the twin puncture wounds as Fletcher held out a tobacco leaf to me which I immediately put in my mouth and chewed. I didn't know if this worked or not but Elisi swore that the tobacco stopped any absorption of the deadly venom in my mouth.

After about a minute, nearly gagging from the bitter taste, I turned my head and politely spit the chewed leaf into my cupped palm. Fletcher gave me his handkerchief and I wrapped the leaf in it then traded him the cloth-wrapped bundle for the jug of moonshine.

I looked at Gerald as I uncorked the jug. "This may sting, Gerald, but we have to get it clean before I can help you."

He squinted his eyes closed and reached out to grasp his mama's hand. I looked at Mr. Davis and said, "You and Fletch hold him down. We don't want him moving around too much until I get some of the poison out."

As Fletcher positioned himself to place his hands on Gerald's ankles and Mr. Davis shifted so he could hold the boy's shoulders, I studied the wound, already starting to swell and turning a purplish shade. I took another deep breath, knowing this next part was going to hurt him. This was the part of healing I hated.

Gerald's eyes were still closed when I tipped the jug over the bite but they flew open as soon as the liquor hit his skin.

His mouth opened and he howled like a wolf. His mama started crying and tried to shush him. "Let him yell if it helps." I looked at Fletch. "Hold him as still as you can." Fletcher nodded.

As quickly as I could, I slashed the skin from just above one of the punctures to just below the other one, and before Gerald could even draw a breath to scream, did the same in the other direction so that I had an X on his leg. Leaning over, putting my mouth to the wound, I sucked as hard as I could, drawing in the coppery taste of blood mingled with a hint of Pa Elliott's best moonshine and, I dearly hoped, the poisonous venom with it. I turned my head, spit on the ground, then placed my mouth over the wound again and repeated the process.

After several minutes, when I deemed I'd done all I could, I looked up. "Did someone make the coffee?"

A hand offered a cup to me over my shoulder. I grasped it, looked to check the strength, noting the dark color. With snake bite, the stronger the better.

"Oh, sugar," I said, remembering. "It needs lots of sugar."

"I added sugar, Bessie, four heaping spoonfuls," Olivia Cross said.

"All right, thank you, Olivia." I turned back to Mrs. Davis. "Would you lift his head so he can drink this? It's nothing but strong coffee with some sugar."

She nodded, taking the cup. Mr. Davis lifted their son's shoulders and leaned him back against his wife's breast. She held the steaming cup to Gerald's mouth. He slurped the hot liquid and grimaced, pushing the cup away. "It's too hot, Ma."

She blew on the cup again then put it right back under his nose. "Hot or cold, you have to drink it, Gerald."

Laying my hand on his shoulder, I said, "It's important, Gerald. You need to drink that and keep drinking it for the rest of the day. The stronger the better and with plenty of sugar. You might not be able to sleep tonight but the coffee will help clear the venom out of your blood."

"Yes, ma'am. I'll try."

Fletcher knelt down beside me and gently swiped his handkerchief over my mouth. It came away tinged with red. I wanted to shudder but held myself still and did my best to smile at Mrs. Davis. "He'll be all right now if you want to go ahead and take him home, but come inside first and I'll give you some dried Calendula. Steep it into a tea, soak a cloth and apply it to help fight infection. I'll also give you a salve of Old Man's Beard which you can use after the wound dries, it'll ease the soreness. Do you know where there's a Pale Indian Plantain plant and can you get some of the leaves?"

She nodded as I went on, "You'll want to bruise a leaf, just sort of crush it in your hand, but not until the juice runs, then bind it over the wound and change it every couple of hours for the first two days to draw out the rest of the poison. After it starts to scab over, use the Old Man's Beard. Be sure to keep him quiet for the next few days, don't let him move around much and don't let him eat anything solid for the rest of today or tomorrow. But give him plenty of strong coffee or tea if he prefers. In a couple of days, he should be fine with something light, maybe cornbread and buttermilk or some broth or soup. And he can move around more but don't let him overdo."

She nodded again and turned back to tend to her boy. Mr. Davis put his hand out and shook Fletcher's. "We thank you and your missus, Fletcher." He took off his hat and scratched his head as he looked at me. I sensed he wanted to say something but couldn't quite form the words.

I smiled and patted his arm. "Your boy will be fine, Mr. Davis. Might've been worse if the snake had gotten him in the early spring. Their venom is more potent then." I looked up at the bright summer sun. "But being mid-summer, I'd say that old snake was about used up for the year." I knew the first part of that statement to be true but had no idea if the last part was correct or not. I only wanted to see the fear leave his eyes.

His lips curved slightly and he gave me a curt nod. "I thank-ee for that, Missus Bessie." He jammed his hat back on his head and addressed Fletcher. "I guess we better be gettin' on now. I'll go hitch up my mule."

Fletcher took his arm and led him away but not before touching his hand to the small of my back. It was, I knew, a small sign of approval, that he appreciated what I'd been able to do.

"I'll go get the Calendula and salve, Mrs. Davis," I said.

She nodded and wiped her hand over her eyes. "I don't...I don't know how I can ever thank you enough, Miss Bessie. You saved my boy and I..." The tears overwhelmed her and she covered her mouth as she sobbed.

I knelt beside her and put my arm around her shoulders. "Hush, now, your boy's going to be fine. He'll have some pain but he's a strong healthy boy and he'll get through it." I looked down at Gerald and noted the color was back in his cheeks. "You do as I said, Gerald, and don't go gallivanting around and worrying your mama, you hear?"

"Yes, Miss Bessie. I will."

"Good." I patted Mrs. Davis on the shoulder. "I predict he'll be right as rain in a few days."

Later, after everyone left, Fletcher and I stood on our small back porch and looked at our "new" barn. I took his hand and smiled at him. "It turned out right nice, don't you think?"

He smiled back. "Almost as good as your papa's in Hot Springs." He squeezed my hand. "Come on, Bess, I want to show you something."

He pulled me off the porch and led me into the cool interior of the barn. I took a deep breath, enjoying the smell of fresh-cut lumber and hay. No horses or cows yet but that would come soon. Fletcher helped me start up the ladder to the loft then followed behind.

I gasped when I reached the top and saw that Fletcher had put a small desk, chair, brand new journal and even an oil lamp to light one dark corner. Hurrying over to it, I ran my hand over the smooth wood then pulled out the chair and sat down, turning to beam a smile over my shoulder at him.

Once again, he'd known what was in my heart and had done his best to give it to me. A feeling of love flowed over me.

"This is wonderful, Fletch. How did you know?"

He shrugged. "Somethin' you said to Ma about missing your corner of the loft at home."

"I did? I don't remember that."

"She asked you what you missed most about Hot Springs and you said other than your family, it was spending time alone in the hay loft. You told her that sometimes it was the only place you felt like yourself, without anyone to pull at you or looking to you for guidance. You said it was just you and God up there and no one else."

I looked down at the desk as the conversation came back to me. Ma Elliott and I had been stringing leather-britches in her sunny kitchen. I had just returned to the Elliotts' house after a hard week at school, staying in the home of one of the rowdiest families in Cedar Creek where I'd felt like I hadn't had a minute to myself all week long.

Standing up, I kissed his cheek and hugged him. "Thank you." When I stepped back, I laughed. "I think I might not be the only one in this family with...um, uncanny knowing."

He smiled. "Sometimes all it takes is paying attention to the people you love to know what they want."

And there it was again, Fletcher telling me he loved me without actually saying the words. It was to be a recurring theme in our married life.

CHAPTER THREE

Summer 1906

They ate supper before they said grace.

A week or two after the barn gathering, I woke up knowing something was going to happen that day. I wasn't sure exactly what but had a feeling someone needed my help so I hurried Fletcher out the door after breakfast, hoping she wouldn't arrive until he'd gotten off the path that wound from the main road and through the trees to our house.

This was to be the way the gift worked for many years— a feeling, an inkling that something was going to happen, or had already happened, but no ironclad facts. Of course, when you're dealing with an ethereal gift such as mine, I suppose that was the way it had to be. I suspect if the feelings came as facts, I probably wouldn't be able to deal with them and indeed might have even lost my sanity at some point.

I wasn't sure who my visitor would be but sensed it was a woman and had a feeling about why she wanted to see me.

As soon as Fletch left, I went to the kitchen and knelt before one of the two small jelly safes he had made for me from some of the lumber he cut. There were only a few jars of wild strawberry jam in one, gifts from Fletcher's mother, as nothing else was ripe enough to make jelly with yet and without a cook stove I didn't feel confident enough to attempt canning anything. In the other, I stored my dried herbs and plants. Soon, when the rest of the fruit came in, the little cabinets would be so full I'd have to find somewhere else to store my herbs and concoctions. The grape vines out by the barn were hanging full as were the pear and apple trees. The woods were full of wild elderberry bushes, blackberry and raspberry brambles and crabapple trees. I hoped to use them all to make jellies and jams, and jars of sliced fruit to sweeten up our winter fare and give us a taste of summer during the cold months ahead.

But for now, the jars at the very edge of the top shelf contained dried Joe Pye weed, Poke berries, Calendula, ginseng roots, and beech bark, all items that could be used for many common illnesses or wounds and all hiding what waited behind. Taking out the jars and setting them on top of the cabinet, I reached to the back for the tins of Queen Anne's Lace seeds and Jack in the Pulpit roots. Both were effective ways of preventing a woman from conceiving if used correctly.

I opened the tin of Queen Anne's Lace, shook out a few of the seeds and popped them into my own mouth, grimacing at the strong taste. It was only right, I suppose, given that I was doing this without my husband's knowledge. I knew I would have to tell him at some point but hadn't yet found the right time or place to broach the subject. It was deceitful but I just couldn't bear the thought of having children at that time in my life. I felt called to teach and knew if I became pregnant there was a better than even chance I'd lose my position. The administrators of McDowell County's school board were all males, and while they preferred their teachers to be married and settled, they did not want them swelling with child.

I frowned at the restrictions men placed all too often on the female sex at that time and wondered if that would ever change. Would women in the future be allowed the same rights as men? Would we ever be allowed to vote? Would we ever be allowed to dictate what happened with our own bodies? I knew there were women working to secure that right for us but doubted seriously they'd ever win that battle. Just as they wouldn't ever attain—

I jumped at the knock on my kitchen door and sighed as I stared through the window. Mattie Gleason, wearing a shawl over her blonde hair as if to disguise herself. It wasn't really a surprise to see her, she'd just given birth three months ago to her seventh child and I imagined she didn't want another one, at least not anytime in the near future. Bless her heart, you could see the toll having so many children in such a short time had taken in the shadows under her eyes, made all the darker by her pale complexion and gaunt cheekbones. Her arms looked so thin I worried they would break with the weight of the baby she held.

Setting both tins on the table, I walked over and opened the door. "Why, hello, Mattie. How nice of you to visit." I stepped back and motioned her inside. "Won't you come in?"

She hesitated, her eyes darting to the right and left as if checking to make sure no one had seen her approaching my house. Meeting my gaze for only an instant, she then peered anxiously over my shoulder, trying to see if there was anyone in the house, I assumed.

"We're alone, Mattie. Fletcher's gone to Old Fort to pick up my new cook stove and won't be back until this afternoon. You come on in here and we'll have us some coffee, or I have herb tea, if you prefer." I looked down at the baby and smiled "I've been meaning to come by and meet the new member of your family but haven't had a chance." I held out my arms. "Can I hold him?"

Without waiting for her answer, I slipped the baby out of her arms. Mattie startled then and her eyes finally landed on mine. I could see the desperation in them and took her hand, leading her to a seat at my kitchen table. I settled in the chair next to her, knowing it would take some coaxing to get the request out. Though I didn't really need her to tell me anymore; I knew the moment I'd seen her standing on my back porch.

I looked down at the swaddled baby sleeping peacefully in my arms. "He sure is a handsome little fella'. What did you name him?" Mattie didn't answer and I searched my mind for the name I'd heard from one of the women at church. "Was it Troy or am I not remembering correctly?"

She still didn't say anything and I fanned my hand in front of my face. "Sure is turning out to be a hot summer, don't you think? Wouldn't it be grand if I had me one of those fancy iceboxes and an iceman to bring me some ice every day like they do in the big cities? 'Course we have our sweet spring water that stays cold year-round and I reckon that's good enough for me. Would you like some water or something else, Mattie?"

She shook her head. "Mrs. Elliott," she started then clamped her mouth shut and looked down at her hands, clasped tight on the table. Her knuckles stood out white and shiny like the ice I'd been speaking of to put her at ease.

I put my hand over hers. "It's all right, Mattie, and please, would you call me Bessie? We're friends, aren't we?"

She nodded but still didn't say anything. She couldn't be much more than my age and yet she already had five boys and two girls. I wondered how old she'd been when she wed. They married young on the mountain, I knew, sometimes before they were old enough to be out of school. Why, I'd heard tell of one of the Moffitt girls marrying at the age of fourteen. 'Course that was due more to her papa's shotgun than anything else.

I reached over behind me and snagged one of the tins, setting it on the table in front of her. "I expect this is what you came for, Mattie. It's Jack in the Pulpit roots. You'll want to grind them into a fine powder, then once a week stir a teaspoon of the powder into cold water. Let it sit for a minute then strain it through some clean cheesecloth and drink it. It won't taste very good but it should keep the babies away."

Her eyes flew to mine, tears brimming. She gulped air, trying to stifle the sobs before they could tear free of her throat.

I patted her hand. "Oh, Mattie, there's no sin in it and don't you think it should be your choice since it's your body which I imagine could use the rest after seven babies. And if you change your mind and decide you're ready for another one, then all you have to do is quit drinking the water. No one but you needs to know about this, not even your husband if you think it best not to tell him."

She pulled a handkerchief out of her sleeve, wiped the tears away. "Oh, I can't tell him." She firmed her lips, "I *won't* tell him. I dasn't, you know how men are, he'd pitch a dyin' duck fit."

I smiled at that. Yes, I knew very well how men were. I'd seen them puff up like a popover because their wife was carrying. As if it was any hardship for the man to get them that way. They never thought about the wear and tear on the woman's body or the fact that she'd just gotten one weaned and out of diapers and in a few months would have to begin the cycle all over again, or that morning sickness, swollen ankles, having to run to the outhouse every thirty minutes, and then the birth of the child would weaken them to the point they became a mere shadow of their former self. Or be so unhappy over their perceived lost lives, their children would pay the price, and a horrible price it could be.

I didn't expect men like her husband to agree with me, and if they ever found out, I'd probably be ostracized at the very least, jailed at the very worst, but I was willing to take that chance, even to the point of keeping it from my own husband which often left me feeling a bit dishonest.

Mattie cleared her throat as she tucked the tin into her apron pocket before reaching for her baby. "I thank you for this, Mrs., uh, Bessie. And I bet if he could talk, Troy would thank you, too. Lawd-a-mercy, it's hard enough with seven young'uns. I just couldn't face having another one right now."

I jiggled the baby's foot. "That tin should be enough to last you a good three or four months. Are you familiar with the Jack in the Pulpit plant?"

She nodded. "They's some grows by the pond on our property. I can dig some of the roots there."

"All right. When you dig them, put them in a sunny spot and let them dry, but only partly else they'll lose their effectiveness. If they dry out completely, toss them out and dig some more."

"Yes'm, Bessie, I'll be sure to do that." She stood up then surprised me when she leaned down and kissed my cheek. "I don't know how to thank you. I'm sure glad Elsa May told me to come see you. She said you saved little

Gerald Davis from that rattlesnake bite and she'd bet her life you'd know what to do about this."

I smiled. I'd have to remember to tell Elisi that I had been accepted, for the most part, by the mountain people as a healer of sorts. And everything I knew was thanks to her.

I told her I was glad I could help her as she went out the door then watched her through the glass as she headed toward the road. Was it my imagination or were her steps lighter now?

The satisfied smile on my face didn't last long. Thoughts of how the men on the mountain would react if they ever found out I was helping their wives not have babies quickly intruded on my self-assurance. And what would Fletcher say if he knew I was deliberately trying not to get pregnant?

As a panacea to my guilty conscience over keeping secrets from my husband, I grabbed the bucket by the door and went out to the well to fill it with water so I could scrub down my kitchen while Fletcher was gone to fetch our new cook stove. I'd spent the last couple of months cooking over the fireplace because the house didn't have a stove when we moved in. At first, I'd thought of it as an adventure, a challenge to be met, but it didn't take long before I saw it as an added chore and insisted we buy a cook stove so I could cook a proper meal. I'd ordered it from the Sears and Roebuck catalogue and it seemed like it took a year for it to get here but it was really only a matter of a couple of weeks. While we waited, Fletcher built a chimney in the kitchen so we wouldn't burn the house down in our desire to feed our stomachs. He had worked on it for over a week and left a huge mess that I had at first cleaned up every day. After the third day, I'd left it till he finished and was out of the house. It was just easier to do things like that when he was gone.

"Bessie, where are you?" Fletcher yelled from the front of the house.

I was on my hands and knees in the kitchen, scouring the floor and singing to make the hated chore a bit more pleasant.

I straightened up, pressing my hands into my aching

back. "In the kitchen," I yelled back. When he appeared in the doorway, I glanced at his feet and sighed. "Don't track that mud in here, Fletcher Elliott."

He looked down at his boots then back up at me with a sheepish grin on his face. "Come see what I've got out in the wagon."

I dumped the brush in the bucket, splashing dirty water on my clean floor. "Is it my cook stove?"

He smiled. "It is, and it's a beaut."

I ran across the wet floor in my stocking feet. "A beautiful stove? You're just dreaming about hot biscuits for breakfast."

"Yep, breakfast and supper and lunch and maybe in between, too."

I shook my head at him. "You better learn to make biscuits then."

He put his arm around my waist and led me over to the door. "How do you know I don't already know how? Maybe Ma taught me when I was a boy."

I shook my head at that. Fletcher cooking? He was a handy man to have around when it came to fixing things but cooking? That would be something to see.

He smiled. "One of these days I might surprise you, Miss Bessie."

I laughed as we went out on the front porch then stopped and gaped at my new stove. Fletcher was right, it was beautiful. I clasped my hands together. It seemed a little silly to get so excited over a hulking piece of cast iron but I knew it would make my chores easier and it was a definite improvement in our life.

I whirled around and hugged Fletcher, almost causing him to lose his balance. He stepped back even as his arms went around me and when he steadied picked me up and swung me in a circle. Breathless and laughing, I held on tight, my arms banded around his neck, my feet swinging free.

When he set me on my feet again, I grabbed his hand and pulled him down to the wagon. "Help me up, Fletch, I want to get a closer look at this beauty."

He caught my waist and boosted me into the wagon bed.

I ran my hands over the smooth cast iron, opened the oven door, and inspected every one of the little holes on the top which allowed the heat to escape so the food could cook. I laughed when I stuck my fingers into the warming bin on the side.

When I turned back to my husband, he was smiling. "Soon as Pa and Tom get here, we'll get her unloaded and hooked up and then you can cook us some supper."

"Why do we have to wait? Can't we get it down ourselves?"

He shook his head. "That thing's as heavy as two horses, maybe three. Ain't no way you and I could do it, 'sides," he turned and looked up the road, "they're already here."

Sure enough, I could hear the clop-clop of horses coming down the hard-packed dirt road and in a matter of seconds saw Pa Elliott and Fletcher's brother Tom in a wagon heading toward the short drive leading to our house. They turned, crossed the small bridge over the creek that ran in front of the house and pulled up beside us.

I looked down at my stocking feet, felt the blush rise in my cheeks. What would Fletcher's father think of me, running around without my shoes in the middle of the day? It wasn't proper and I tugged on my dress to make it a little longer but that didn't work. I shrugged. Too late to worry about it now. Besides I'd lived with the man and his wife for over five years. Knowing Pa Elliott, he wouldn't even notice.

Fletcher jumped out of the wagon and turned to lift me down before he greeted his family as they alit from their wagon. I said hello then excused myself and ran back into the house to get my shoes. When I came back out on the porch, Tom and Fletcher had scooted the stove as far as possible to the edge of the wagon bed and were getting ready to lift it down.

"Can I help?" I asked.

Tom looked at me and grinned. "I'm right sure Fletch and I can handle it, Moonfixer. You just stand there and look pretty."

I gave him a smile of my own. All the mountain people

had taken to calling me Moonfixer because they said I was "right-tall for a woman." Pa Elliott started it the first time I met him and it wasn't long before everyone was calling me that. I wasn't anywhere near tall enough to reach up and fix the moon, of course, but the fact that I had a nickname among these people made me feel as if they accepted me into their midst.

Fletcher frowned as his father reached into the other wagon and pulled a jug of moonshine from underneath the bench seat. He didn't approve of drinking and often tried to talk his father into doing something other than tending his still and selling the whiskey to the people who lived on the mountain.

Pa Elliott's standard answer to that was that all the men would come after him and force him to make his whiskey if he didn't do it already. He was proud of his reputation as the "best moonshiner in these parts" and took an equal amount of pride in the fact that he'd never been shut down. Of course, the sheriff and most of his deputies were regular customers and the federal government couldn't "find their hind-ends with a map", as Pa Elliott said, so he didn't have much to worry about.

"Wouldn't it be easier to take the wagon around the back and take the stove in the kitchen door?" I asked.

"It would but I'm not sure we can trust those steps," Fletcher said as he rolled up his sleeves.

Our little house was in a constant state of repair these days. Built long before the Civil War for the Overseer and his family to live in, it had been vacant for many years after the war ended. Fletcher and I had spent the first weeks of the summer scrubbing, hammering, building up or tearing down. It was small, only four rooms, and still needed a lot of work but at least we could live there without fear of falling through the floors or catching some unknown disease or dodging raindrops when it rained.

I retreated to a corner of the porch as Fletcher and Tom grasped the stove and hoisted it up the steps. Muscles straining, they continued on into the house, through the small living room and into the kitchen in back. Pa and I followed along behind, Pa offering tips his sons mostly ignored. When they scooted the heavy stove into place, Fletcher took his bandanna out of his back pocket and wiped his brow.

Tom did the same. "I hope that's where you want it, Moonfixer, 'cause that heavy mother-lovin' son of a gun ain't going anywhere anytime soon."

I laughed. "It doesn't need to go anywhere, it just needs to cook. Can we start a fire, Fletch?"

"Not till I get the chimney pipe attached and then we'll get her going."

Pa sat down at the kitchen table, took out his pipe but didn't light it, only chewed on the stem as he watched his sons do the work. I sat down beside him and chatted with Tom about his wife, Laura, pregnant with their third child, and his two little girls. I also asked Fletcher's father about his wife and other children. Everyone was doing fine and we all agreed this was turning out to be one of the hottest summers we'd ever known.

It wasn't long before Fletcher had the pipe attached. I watched as he added some kindling and lit it, blowing on it to get it going good. When he had a good flame, he reached for one of the split logs I'd brought in that morning, placing it on top. The fire caught and I clapped my hands and restrained myself from dancing a jig. Instead, I got busy preparing a pot of coffee, grinding the beans in the grinder mounted on top of the jelly safe and thinking how good that wild strawberry jam and the butter I'd churned fresh that morning would taste on hot biscuits baked in my new oven.

And maybe after Fletcher's father and brother were gone, I'd grab Fletcher's hands and together we'd dance that jig with our bellies full of food prepared on my new stove.

CHAPTER FOUR

Late Summer 1906

He's crooked-er than a $3 bill.

The long, hot summer was winding down, occasionally giving up its claim to hot, dry weather and teasing us with a taste of the cool, windy days that lay ahead. But this day had been a particularly brutal one, the sun blaring down hot and fierce without a cloud in the sky or a breeze to cool the skin. After supper, Fletcher and I retreated to the front porch, hoping the air would chill as the sun made its descent behind the mountains to our west. I sat in a chair, somewhat lethargically listening to my husband expand on what he planned to do with our farm, hoping he would be able to accomplish everything he wanted to. I spied a figure in the distance walking down the roadway and leaned forward, squinting my eyes, curious if I knew the person and were they coming to pay us a visit.

Fletcher, noticing this, gazed that way. "Looks to be a stranger, Bess," he said.

As Fletcher and I watched the short, squat man amble up the pathway to our house, I wondered what business drove him here but Fletcher apparently had a good idea. "Better hang on to your petticoat, Bessie girl," he said with a growl, "we got us a politician coming our way."

The man walked like a duck, swaying from side to side, and as he grew nearer, I couldn't help but think the name might well fit him with his small, dark beady eyes, nose which took up most of his face, and receding chin. With a sly grin, he stepped on the porch, taking off his hat and mopping sweat off his brow with a soggy handkerchief. "Good evening to you," he said with a slight bow. He wore what little remained of his gray hair slicked back with what I assumed must be some sort of pomade although it smelled to me like bear grease. The halo of bare skin on the crown of his head was so shiny, I wondered if I could see myself in it as he leaned toward me, and if I reached out and touched it, would that skin be as smooth and soft as a baby's leg?

Fletcher nodded a greeting as I returned to my seat. I had no interest in a politician trying to weasel money out of us for whatever intent he had.

"Sure is hot this time of year," the man said.

"Sure is," Fletcher said.

He held out his hand to Fletcher. "Name's Orson Belle."

Fletcher returned the handshake, saying, "Fletcher Elliott and this here's my wife Bessie."

"Pleased to meet you, Mr. Elliott." He darted a quick glance at me, barely inclining his head. "Ma'am." He returned his gaze to Fletch. "You mind if I sit down, rest my feet for a bit?"

Fletcher gestured with his hand for the man to take his seat and went to lean against the porch rail.

"Whoo-wee, this humidity is somethin' else," Mr. Belle said, fanning his perspiring face with his hat.

I looked down at my lap as I wrinkled my nose. The air moving in my direction smelled of sour sweat and the bear grease I was now sure he'd used on his hair.

"What can we do for you, Mr. Belle?" Fletcher's face remained impassive but his voice implied impatience and irritation.

"Well, now, I've come here for a good reason and that's to talk to you about the upcoming election to the state legislature."

My eyes met Fletcher's, whose gleamed with amusement, and I tipped my head toward him, my acknowledgement of his earlier call.

We watched as Mr. Belle took off his coat and laid it

across his knees. He leaned back in the chair, settling in. Not for long, I thought.

The foul stench intensified and I wished for a handkerchief to hold over my nose. The man smelled as if he hadn't bathed in a month of Sundays.

"Well, now, Mr. Elliott, I think you can agree with me, this state is in dire straits. And things ain't gonna change unless we get the right kind of folks in the state legislature to ensure that we get ourselves headed in the right direction." He paused, as if waiting for some response but Fletcher remained silent.

He leaned back, rocking the chair a bit, and hooked his thumbs under his suspenders, sliding them up to his shoulder then down to the top of his britches. The straps of his gallowses were bright red to match his shirt, the only things colorful about this man who seemed all neutral to me with his gray hair, sallow complexion and brown suit. I watched as his thumbs traveled this same route over and over again and wondered what sort of comfort he took from this.

The movement of his thumbs stopped and he leaned toward us. "You declared yourself politically, Mr. Elliott?" His beady eyes now reminded me of a wild boar, mean with the need for blood, ready to thrust his head down and bore someone or something.

"My wife and I don't involve ourselves in politics," Fletcher said.

"Well, now, maybe you do and maybe you don't, but if'n you don't, it's about time you did, and for the right party, too."

"I don't vote for any party, I vote for the man best suited to the job." Fletcher stared at the red suspenders for a long moment. I watched his eyes harden as he said, "You're a Democrat."

Mr. Belle straightened in his chair. "Yes, sir, I am, and I'm sure hoping you ain't one of those damned Republicans or Populists. If so, it's my duty to convince you otherwise."

I wished Papa was here to set this man straight. He was a Democrat but never saw it as his duty to convince anyone they were in the wrong no matter what party they belonged to although he often declared he wouldn't let a Republican past the front gate. I tried to hold my tongue but couldn't keep from saying, "I don't see that you have any business here, Mr. Belle. My husband told you we don't involve ourselves politically."

He ignored me, leaning back in the chair again, and began that same movement with the thumbs beneath the suspenders.

It was all I could do to keep my hands from waving in front of my face so I could get a breath of fresh, unfettered air.

"Well, now, the way I see it, Mr. Elliott, each and every man in this county needs to step up and vote and make hisself count. Now, I'm running on the Democratic party for a position at the state legislature and I'd like to ask for your vote."

My fists clinched. Why in the world women didn't have the same right to vote as men was beyond me. There had been talk of the women's suffrage movement for greater than half a century but in our part of the country it was only discussed as a possible rumor. I vowed if it got to North Carolina, I'd be one of the women not only supporting it but demanding it.

Fletch eyed the red suspenders again. "You one of them yellow-dawg Democrats?"

Those beady eyes almost lost themselves in the folds of his eyes. "I take offense at that term, sir. I'm a Democrat, pure and simple." He straightened up, as proud as a peacock. "Why, I've even got Furnifold Simmons backing me." When neither of us responded, he said, "You know who that is, don't you?"

Fletcher spat in the yard. "I hear they call him the Great White Father."

Mr. Belle nodded. "The very man. And it's his intention to see to it that this state becomes one of the best in the nation. And he means to start by taking power away from the niggers, getting 'em out of political office and ending negro domination afore it gets started. As you know, only white men are fit to hold office."

Fletcher shook his head. "I don't reckon the color of one's skin has anything to do with politics or who's the fittest to do anything."

"Not according to Fernifold Simmons. Why, he's probably one of the most powerful men in North Carolina right now and bound to—"

"He's a vengeful, biased man who hates anybody that ain't the color he is, pure and simple," Fletcher said, his voice hard. "And if you got him backing you, you're one, too, and I think it'd be best if you get off my land and don't come back. I ain't got use for men who think God gave them the right to be judge, jury and executioner of a black man simply because he argues with a white man."

"Well now, if you're referring to that lynching awhile back, maybe you didn't get the full story."

"I don't care to hear your side of it, Mr. Belle. I'm asking you to leave. If you don't, I'll personally escort you off my land." Fletcher stood his full height and I thought what a grand specimen of a man he was with his wide shoulders, strong arms and legs.

"You might regret saying those words to me," Mr. Belle said, his fleshy jowls flushing bright red.

"What you gonna do, put on one of those red shirts, come here, burn my barn, put a cross in my yard and burn it like the KKKs do? The likes of you don't scare me one bit, Mr. Belle, and if I decide to vote in the upcoming election, it won't be for the likes of you and that evil Furnifold Simmons."

When Mr. Belle made no attempt to move, Fletcher stepped toward him and that was all it took. He gathered up his coat and hat and hurried off the porch. As we watched him duck walk back to the road, I slipped my hand in Fletcher's. "I'm mighty proud of you, husband."

"If he gets some red shirts together and comes back, you might not feel so inclined, Bess," Fletcher said, turning to me.

"I will, no matter what," I said, kissing him. "You might want to let your chair air for a bit before you sit down again." I grinned and held my nose. "Lord-a-mercy, I haven't smelled anything that bad since that polecat crawled under the house and died."

Fletcher laughed and planted a smacking kiss on my lips.

CHAPTER FIVE

Late Summer 1906

He ain't got the good sense God gave a billy goat.

Since I'd come to live on the mountain, I'd taught at Cedar Creek then Crooked Creek, both one-room schools with me as the only teacher and both so far away from the Elliotts' house that I'd had to board with one or another of my students' families during the week. I saw Fletcher only on the weekends or holidays and, of course, during the summers when school was out. I learned much from those two positions and approached my new job at Cedar Grove School with confidence, eager to meet my students and start the upcoming school year which would be so much better than the past. My new school was an easy walk to and from our small farm which I had christened Cedar Creek Farm for the branch of Cedar Creek that flowed through our front yard, and I looked forward to returning to my own home at the end of the day.

A week before school officially started, Fletcher borrowed a neighbor's wagon and drove me to see my new place of employment. I gathered my school supplies – a few books, a box of chalk, and a notebook for the class roll – and placed them under the seat of the wagon. I also packed a lunch for us in case it took more than a few hours to get set up. Fletcher brought a hammer, some nails, and a saw so that he could take care of any simple repairs that may be needed.

Although still a few weeks away if you went by the calendar, fall seemed determined to shove summer out of its way as if they were two children waging a schoolyard battle for power. And like a petulant child, when fall lost the fight, it would gather up its toys, cool breezes and wisps of mountain fog floating among the trees, and trudge home around midmorning, leaving summer to play alone for the rest of the day.

The chilly morning proved to be a harbinger for the much colder weather that would soon be upon us, our breath clouding the air as we rode along in the brisk breeze that had me wishing I'd brought along a blanket to spread across our laps. It made me think of the trip Papa and I had taken on another fall day to collect taxes, the one when Mr. Sullivan had given Papa a sewing machine in lieu of the taxes he owed and where I had actually seen the children of a Melungeon and learned these people were not the boogey-men parents threatened their children with

Fletcher brought me out of my memories when he said, "Look there, Bessie." He pointed to a tree limb hanging over the creek. As we passed by, Fletcher whistled a tune and the mockingbird perched on the limb immediately answered him in kind, as if heralding our presence.

"He's welcoming you to Cedar Grove," Fletcher said.

I laughed. "Not a very warm welcome but I'll take it."

The fog was heavier around the creek, almost seeming to wrap us in a cold, damp blanket, and I scooted over on the bench seat closer to Fletcher. Thinking of Papa, I said, "That fog means we're going to have a heavy snow come this winter."

Fletcher nodded. "Makes me think of ghosts the way it drifts and gathers in clumps that way." He smiled. "Reminds me of my cousin Lewis, too."

"Cousin Lewis? Have I met him?"

"I don't think you have, he lives way to the other side of the mountain. Ol' Lewis is getting pretty long in the tooth and he doesn't get out much anymore."

"But why does the fog remind you of him?'

He laughed again and I joined with him even though I didn't have any idea what he was talking about. Knowing the mountain people, this was bound to be good.

"Some years back, oh, maybe fifteen, twenty years ago – I was just a boy when this happened – it seems ole Lewis was out one night doing some hunting. It started to rain, and since he wasn't having much luck with his hunting, he decided to go on back home. The quickest way was through the cemetery at the church but Lewis, well, let's just say he's got a fanciful imagination so he really didn't want to go through the cemetery, but right about then, the storm started whipping the wind and pouring water like it was coming from buckets so he decided he'd try it after all.

"He got about halfway through when he heard a sound and looked back over his shoulder to where ol' Rattlesnake Hudgins is buried. Rattlesnake used to be pretty famous here on the mountain for his mean ways and he was the reason Lewis didn't want to go through the cemetery 'cause people say Rattlesnake keeps watch and chases off anyone who dares to trespass there at night and disturb his eternal sleep.

"Well, Lewis, with his fanciful imagination, claims that night when he turned to look, he saw a white shape come out of the ground right over ol' Rattlesnake's grave and he took off running fast as he could. He ran clear up to Polecat Holler and on to the gap at Whistling Spring but that white shape stayed right with him, floating along behind no matter how fast he ran.

"He finally had to stop to catch his breath and sat himself down on a big log. The ghost floated right up and settled next to him on that log. Lewis was scared out of his mind and says he almost fainted when Rattlesnake cackled out a laugh and then spoke to him, saying 'We's come a long ways, h'ain't we, boy?'"

I laughed. "And what did cousin Lewis do?"

"Well, Lewis, he probably ran like the devil was after him, but what he says he did was he answered back, 'Yep, we sure have, and when I rest awhile, we're going again.' When he got his breath, or so he claims, he outran Rattlesnake and made it home safely to his bed."

Fletcher looked at me and smiled when I shook my head. "What do you think really happened?"

"Well, since I've never heard tell of ol' Rattlesnake rising out of the ground, I think what Lewis saw was just a blob of fog that the wind blew in his direction. Lewis thought he'd seen a ghost but all he saw was a trick of these ol' mountains. Aunt Mintie Jane said he showed up at the house looking like he'd seen a ghost and pale as one, too. He was shaking like the leaves on the trees during a storm and wouldn't say a word, just took to his bed and pulled the covers over his head and stayed there for a full day."

I smiled at that image. "Poor Lewis. Sounds like he's got about as much sense as Tommy Bearing."

Fletcher laughed. "At least he didn't shoot the ghost like Tommy did."

"And end up shooting his neighbor's white mule instead. I wonder if Mr. Morris ever forgave him for that one?"

"Doubt it. Morris could be as crotchety as they say ol' Rattlesnake Hudgins was when he was alive."

"You didn't know him?"

"Nope, he died a long time ago, long before I was a gleam in my pa's eye as Ma would say, but I've heard stories about him all my life. All the women say he was as ornery as a striped-eyed rattlesnake which is where he got his name. Not that anybody ever called him that to his face. It was only after he died and started haunting the graveyard that folks started calling him that."

I looked at him in surprise. "Do you believe in ghosts, Fletcher?"

He grinned. "Didn't used to, but as I get older, my mind isn't set so much on having to see something to believe it. You've taught me that, Bess."

"I have?"

"Yep, the way you sometimes know things that you have no way of knowing. You knew Luther Hall was dead before you got the news, didn't you?"

"Yes, I guess I did." I squirmed on the hard wooden bench. "Does that bother you? I mean, that I have Elisi's gift?"

He shook his head. "It doesn't bother me, it's part of who you are. Besides, it might be pretty nice sometimes to know things before they happen."

"Poor Luther. Loney wrote that Evvie showed up at church a few Sundays ago wearing a huge diamond ring. When somebody asked her about it, she said she'd done right by Luther and it was about time he did right by her, too. She sold every drop of moonshine he had put aside, then she sold his still and horse, and after she paid for a small grave stone, she took the train to Asheville and bought herself the biggest diamond she could find. She said Luther got his stone and she figured she deserved one of her own for putting up with him all those years."

"I guess that's one way of looking at it." He flicked the reins. "Looks like we're here," he said as we drove into the clearing around the little one-room schoolhouse.

"Oh, that didn't take hardly any time at all."

"Well, let's see what we've got here." Fletcher pointed at the log building. "Need to fix that door first thing. Its hanging crooked. Might let in the cold."

The door looked perfectly fine to me but I supposed Fletcher knew more about that sort of thing than I did so I smiled at him. "Thank you, Mr. Elliott, I would certainly appreciate that."

He drew on the reins then set the brake on the wagon and hopped down, coming around to help me climb out. I turned and studied the school, the clearing where I knew the children would play at recess, and the outhouse situated around the side. There was a small front porch with a large school bell hanging beside it. I imagined myself tugging on that rope and calling the school day to order.

"Do you think it's all right for us to just go on in?" I asked.

He shrugged as he pulled the package of school supplies from under the seat of the wagon. "Don't know why not, you're the teacher."

I laughed as I squared my shoulders. "Yes, I am, aren't I?"

Holding the package, he took my arm and guided me up

the steps. When I turned the knob, the door swung open with a squeak, dragging slightly on the wood floor as I walked inside, getting my first glance of the place I'd spend the majority of my time for the next nine months. I had expected dust but obviously the womenfolk had taken the time to come in and give the place a good cleaning. There were shelves under a chalkboard on the front wall and a large wooden desk sat in front of smaller desks lined up in rows across the room.

I cleared my throat and tried to ignore the overwhelming feeling I got at the first of every school year; the fact that I would be responsible for shaping the minds of the students who would sit at those desks. What if I failed? What if the students didn't like me? And what if they complained to their parents who could have me fired?

"What's the matter, Bess?" Fletcher asked.

I gripped his hand in mine. "I'm a little nervous."

"What about?"

I shook my head. "It's the same feeling I get every year. I should be used to it by now."

"What kind of feeling?"

I tried to smile. "It's nothing really, just a bit of foolishness I always suffer at the first of every new school year. What if the children all hate me and won't listen to me? What if I'm a failure?"

Fletcher surprised me when he pulled me close and hugged me. "You'll do fine, Bess."

"How can you be so sure?"

"Because I saw what you did with my sister Florie a few years ago. I watched you teach her to read and cipher and she went off to school that year ahead of everyone in her class. Didn't matter a bit that she'd missed most of the year before what with being so sick, she was ahead of all of them. More than that, I know how much you love teaching. I'm pretty sure your students will see that and they'll do their best to learn what you teach them."

I squeezed his hand. Once again, my husband had calmed my fears and made me feel better about myself. "Thank you, Fletcher."

He smiled at me and picked up the wrapped package from where he'd placed it on the corner of the teacher's desk. "I brought you something in honor of your first teaching position where you'll be coming home to me every night instead of staying with one of the families of your students." He shook it and I heard the muffled clang of a metal bell.

"Oh, Fletcher, you got me a school bell." I tore the paper off then ran my hands over the carved wooden handle and down the shiny metal sides of the bell, turning it over to look at the metal clapper inside. "It's beautiful, Fletcher. Thank you."

He pulled his bandana out of his back pocket. "Here, don't cry, it was supposed to make you smile."

I smiled. "These are tears of happiness. I'm a very lucky woman."

He pointed to the front of the room. "Go on up there and try it out. Since I can't be here next Monday morning, I want to see what you look like up there."

I held the bell up and gave it a few good shakes, delighting in the clear ring of the clapper. "It's perfect, Fletcher, thank you so much."

He grinned. "Well, let's check out the rest of the place and see what's what."

We toured the one room slowly. While we were checking the windows, we noticed a rather large hole in the floor underneath one of them.

Fletcher scratched his head. "I wonder how that happened. I can fix it for you, Bess, if you want. I'll have to get some wood first, though."

I laughed. "Mayhap before the winter gets here but I don't see it as a priority right now. We've had a few chilly mornings but the sun always warms it up nicely before long. It can wait."

We lifted the tops of the desks, studied the etchings left by some of the students on top of a couple of them. "Well, at least they know their ABCs," I said. "But I wonder if they know how to put them together to make words and then put the words together to make sentences."

Fletcher rubbed his hand over my shoulder. "If they

don't, you'll teach them."

We walked outside, stopped to examine the small table beside the door with a bucket sitting on top. "Guess that's for water," Fletcher said. "Needs a dipper, though, if you want to use it for drinking water."

"But where would you get the water," I wondered, scanning the area around the school. "I don't see a well anywhere."

"Maybe it's out back." Fletcher took my hand and guided me off the tiny porch and around the side of the school.

There was an outhouse and not much else but dirt until we walked into the trees where we found a small stream not far from the clearing. I nodded when Fletcher said he guessed I could fill the bucket there and have one of the bigger boys carry it to the schoolhouse for me.

I didn't know it then, but that creek would become an important necessity for me once the school year started.

I arrived early on the first day of school, excitement driving me from my bed before sunrise, anticipation at my heels every step of the short walk to Cedar Grove. After filling the bucket at the creek and setting it inside by the stove, I stood on the front stoop, watching my students as they slowly ambled into the schoolyard. Most were in tight knots of other children, siblings and friends. Some I knew and some I didn't. A couple of them stood alone on the outskirts of the group. They all looked a bit apprehensive, more than a little uncertain, and a lot curious. One boy stood with his mother, tightly gripping her hand. One girl and three of the boys stood taller than me and two of the boys looked to be near grown men. I said a silent prayer that I would be able to control them despite their size.

No one seemed anxious to go inside so I reached up and tugged on the rope attached to the bell. All eyes turned to me and I smiled, hoping to put them at ease or at least let them know they were welcome here. I wanted to appear confident though the first day jitters were dancing a merry jig in my stomach.

The woman, a comely young lady whom I imagined had

given the boys a merry chase before she married, walked up to the porch, tugging the little boy behind her. She held a small baby in her arms, swaddled tight in a crocheted pink blanket.

"Mrs. Elliott, I'm Matilda Boswell, welcome to Cedar Grove." She pulled the boy in front of her. "This here's my son, Bobby." She smiled as she wet her fingers and tried to tame the cowlick sticking up at the crown of the boy's head. "He's not for certain he wants to go to school." She lowered her voice. "His pa never went and he's of a mind to be just like his pa."

I looked down at Bobby and gave him a reassuring smile as most of the other students parted like the Red Sea around our little group and walked inside. "Hello, Bobby, I'm Miss Bessie." I had decided to allow the children to call me by my given name, hoping it would eliminate the gap between teacher and student—or at least, narrow it a little. "Is this your first year at school?"

He shrugged, scuffing the toe of his boot in the dirt. His mother answered for him. "Oh no, Mrs. Ell...Miss Bessie, it's his second." She puffed up some and went on. "He can read right well and write some and he can count all the way to a hundred, but he doesn't want to go to school. We had a hard time convincing him this morning that he needs learning more than he needs to stay at home and help his pa."

I crouched down, waited until Bobby's eyes lifted and met mine. Smiling, I said, "You must be very smart. Would you do me a favor, Bobby?"

Some of the apprehension left his eyes as he nodded. "Yes, ma'am," he muttered.

"Thank you. Would you go on in and count how many students we have? Can you do that, please?"

"Yes, ma'am," he said again but didn't move. His mother placed her hand on his shoulder and said, "Go ahead and do as Miss Bessie says, son."

That got his feet moving in a reluctant shuffle up the steps and inside the schoolhouse. I smiled at Mrs. Boswell. "I'm pleased to meet you, Mrs. Boswell, and I'm sure Bobby will be fine."

"He's a good boy but he's more interested in farm work and caring for the animals than he is in reading and writing. Maybe you can change his mind. Well, I'd best be getting home to my chores." She nodded and turned away.

"Don't worry, Mrs. Boswell, we'll be all right. Before you go, you said Bobby was interested in caring for the animals. What's his favorite?"

Turning back toward me, she thought for a few seconds and said, "He likes them all, really, but his favorite seems to be the chickens. Or really, one chicken in particular that he raised from a chick." She laughed. "Law, that silly thing follows Bobby around like a puppy."

I smiled as a picture of Miss Cordy and her pet hen, Elsie, came to my mind. "Thank you, Mrs. Boswell."

She waved over her shoulder. Turning to go inside, I paused a moment, took a deep breath, let it out slowly and squared my shoulders. Thinking of Miss Julia, the principal of Dorland Institute, I walked through the door. Bobby rushed over to me, mumbled, "Twenty-seven," then turned and went to sit down at a desk in the back beside another boy.

All eyes turned to me, watching as I walked to the front of the classroom to stand behind my desk. Smiling, I raised my voice and said, "Good morning, everyone. My name is Miss Bessie and I'm your teacher. Before we get to our studies, I'd like to get to know you all a bit. Please stand and tell me your name, what grade you're in, and what your favorite school subject is when I call on you." I sat down and pointed to Bobby. "Bobby, would you mind starting?"

Bobby blushed but stood and said, "Bobby Boswell, Miss Bessie. I'm in second grade, and I like arithmetic the best."

I noted it down in my notebook. "Thank you, Bobby, you may sit down. I looked at the boy beside him and nodded.

He stood up. "Jimmy Nash, I'm in third grade, and I like history."

We made our way slowly through all of the students. I noted each name, grade, and favorite subject on my paper, keeping a separate tally of the number in each grade. When the last student had introduced herself, I stood up and wrote *Miss Bessie Elliott* on the chalkboard, underlining *Bessie* several times before turning back to the class.

"It's a pleasure to meet all of you. Now, I'd like you all to line up by your grade level, starting with first, second and third over against that wall." I pointed to the far side of the classroom. "Down the center aisle, I want fourth, fifth and sixth. Then against the other wall, seventh and eighth."

Surprised at the lack of horsing around—they must have been more anxious than I thought they would be—I waited as they all filed into their proper groups. Then I studied the arrangement of the desks and decided where to place everyone; second and third, the largest group, on one side of the classroom, fourth and fifth on the opposite side, leaving the middle two rows of desks. I put the youngest students in the front and the oldest and largest, in the back.

When everyone was seated, I walked to the chalkboard and pointed to my name. "This is my name, but it isn't my name." Several mouths fell open, others frowned at me and a couple looked at me like I'd just told them I was the devil himself. I smiled and waited. It didn't take long for a hand to shoot in the air. I consulted my list, found the name and asked, "Yes, Lula?"

"That don't make no sense, uh...Miss Bessie."

"That *doesn't* make sense, Lula." I softened the admonition with a smile, imagining Mama smiling down on me from heaven, approving my unconscious grammar correction, something I'd learned early at her knee. "It isn't supposed to make sense, as it's a riddle. I like riddles and I hope you do, too, because I'll have at least one for you every week. Your job will be to try to figure them out but you can't tell anyone when you do. You must keep it a secret until Friday morning when I will ask you to come up to my desk one by one and tell me your answer."

More frowns. I knew I had to sweeten the pot. "Anyone who gives me the correct answer will be given an extra ten minutes at recess on Friday."

This finally got some smiles and even a few whispers. I clapped my hands together and all those faces turned back to me, showing a great deal more eagerness and interest now.

I spent the rest of the morning assessing the correct placement levels for reading. While I worked with a small group of students, I had the others write out the alphabet so I could assess their writing later. I'd do the arithmetic in the afternoon since that was bound to take longer and was my least favorite subject. At noon, after I finished with the last student, a hulking boy named Luke, I picked up the bell Fletcher had given me and gave it a good shake. "That means it's time for lunch, children. How many of you go home to eat?" Five hands shot up and I nodded. "You may go, but please return in a timely fashion." They stood and I noticed something was wrong but couldn't put my finger on what it was. "Those of you who brought your lunch with you may either eat at your desk or go outside since it's a nice day. I'll ring the bell when it's time to come back in." I watched as a few of the students picked up their lunches to go outside and the rest set their lunch pails on their desks. I still couldn't figure out exactly what was bothering me but pushed it aside and went behind my desk to get my own lunch. Maybe if I filled my grumbling stomach, it would come to me.

The children who stayed inside finished their lunch in a matter of minutes and then started talking amongst themselves. I listened to their chatter, letting my mind wander, wondering what Fletcher was doing which was silly because I knew he was working. He had told me that morning he was going to be cutting lumber and that made me remember him offering to fix the hole in the floor over by the windows on the fourth and fifth grade side of the class. My eyes traveled over in that direction and it finally hit me; the desk right beside the hole had been empty when I rang the bell for lunchtime.

But it hadn't been that morning. In fact, it, or really, the student in it, Peter Elliott, one of Fletcher's many cousins, had been a major source of frustration when I was trying to determine how well he could read and write.

Not very well at all and he didn't show any sign of wanting to better his abilities.

I stood up, walked over to Peter's desk and looked down

at the hole in the floor. It wasn't very large but was it possible he'd gotten tired or bored and decided to slip out through the hole? I crouched down, peered into the darkness beneath the floor and jumped when one of the students spoke behind me.

"Have you figured it out yet, Miss Bessie?"

I looked up into Bobby Boswell's amused eyes.

"Is it a riddle then?"

He nodded. "It sure is but not a hard one. Took t'other teacher almost a month to figure it out and she still didn't believe it until she saw it with her own eyes."

I stood up. "Well, let me see." I held up a finger. "First, Mr. Peter Elliott is sitting in this desk. Second, Mr. Peter Elliott magically disappears sometime after I tested his reading and writing skills but before lunch." I grinned at Bobby. "And third, we have this very convenient hole in the floor right next to his desk. It's a little small but I imagine if a person was determined enough, he could force his way through it to the outside. Then it's only a matter of scooting out from under the schoolhouse and taking off for home."

Bobby shook his head and laughed. "Oh, no, ma'am. He won't go home, Miss Bessie, his ma would skin him alive if she caught him playing hooky again. What he usually does is go down to the creek and look for crawdads or tadpoles or something. That's how he got the name of Slippery Pete."

I had to laugh. If the rest of my students were as wily and sly as Slippery Pete Elliott, it promised to be an interesting and fun year.

CHAPTER SIX

Fall 1906

Scared as a sinner in a cyclone.

Fall settled on the mountain like a woman donning a multihued dress. The trees were alive with color, vivid reds mingling with glowing golds, bright oranges fading into warm browns, all contrasting with the deep greens of the deciduous cedars and pines and framed by a sky so blue it almost hurt the eyes to look at it. October was always a special month in the mountains, a time to celebrate a change of seasons when summer gave over to fall, allowing the mountain folk a respite from heat and haze and the forthcoming ice and snow. The perfect month for my favorite event, molasses-making, mayhap because I first met Fletcher at my Uncle Robert's farm in Walnut when my family traveled there several years earlier to help make molasses.

Beginning in September, whenever mountain folk gathered together, their discourse always turned to debating the right time to harvest the sorghum cane and make molasses, which was a finicky process as the cane had to be picked at just the right time. Too early, green cane made green molasses which was not tasty, and if it frosted before harvesting, the molasses would be bitter. Since molasses making took place only once a year, most families didn't have a grinder but would gather together at the home of a farmer who possessed one and all would pitch in to help. Or if no one had a grinder, an experienced miller would travel from place to place with a portable mill. But on Stone Mountain, Thorney Dalton, Fletcher's pa's fiercest competitor for making moonshine, provided the mill, one he liked to brag he traded a homemade still for, and farmers from as far away as Old Fort came to make molasses.

As it turned out, Thorney picked a good day for grinding the sorghum cane, a sunny Saturday in mid October. Early that morning, I fried two chickens and packed them into a basket with biscuits, jars of elderberry jam, and fried apples while Fletch hitched up our two recently-acquired mules to our wagon. When I stepped outside, I stood on the porch a moment, breathing in the cool air, piquant with the sweet scent of fallen apples and musty odor of decaying leaves. The sky was beginning to lighten over the mountain, the sun making its debut with bright swirls of yellow and green, and I thought it looked to be a beautiful day. Fletch took the basket from me and set it under the seat before helping me up. He climbed in beside me, picked up the reins and clucked to our mules and off we set at a leisurely pace.

I looked in the bed of the wagon, smiling at the cane piled there. Fletch and I planted the sorghum seeds around the middle of May and when the seeds were dark-brown and ready to drop, cut off the stalks and removed the fathers, what the mountain people called the blades. We then cut the stalks to remove the seeds and stood the cane for a week, which we'd been told made the molasses tastier. A sense of pride enveloped me. This had been my first time with sorghum and I discovered a love for harvesting what I planted and watched grow that would stay with me all my life.

When we arrived, Thorney's small, rocky yard was filled with horses, mules and wagons. I didn't see a garden nearby and wondered if he had planted farther up the mountain or perhaps made enough from moonshining that didn't require the necessity of growing food for his family. The house backed up to a ridge rising dark and stony behind it, with a ramshackle barn nearby along with two outhouses, both of which looked to be two-seaters. It was rumored Thorney had so many children, even he had lost count, and I imagined with all their children, that would be a necessity. The house rambled this way and that and appeared to have been pieced together, as if rooms had been added on through the years. Again, I was sure, as a way to make room for their family as it expanded.

I smiled when I saw Thorney surrounded by mountain men, engaged in his favorite pastime, telling tall tales about the revenuers who constantly plagued him. Numerous children accompanied by barking dogs darted in and around the adults, seeming to be having a grand time. I recognized several of my students, along with Thorney's four children who attended school. Other men milled about in groups and I noted women placing food on a long table Thorney had devised by setting wooden planks on large whiskey barrels. After Fletcher helped me down, I joined the women, smiling and nodding at those I knew while unpacking my basket and placing the food on the table. It looked to be a fine spread we'd have come dinnertime.

Everyone quieted when Thorney put his fingers in his mouth and whistled shrilly. As he assigned chores to the men and women and decided the order in which the cane would be milled, I realized Thorney had this down to a science. I was one of the women chosen to skim the sorghum juice, a job which we would do in turns since it would take six hours for it to boil and could be back-breaking work as it must be constantly skimmed. It was important not to burn the sorghum or it would be ruined.

I moved among the women, talking with those I knew and introducing myself to strangers, trying to memorize names to go with faces. Thorney's wife Vera was a surprise. I had expected a small, frail woman worn away by years of producing children but instead found a large, robust woman with heavy breasts and hips, rosy cheeks and a loud laugh. She held one babe in her arms and a toddler clutched her skirts. She smiled at me and said, "I'm mighty pleased to finally meet you, Moonfixer." She stepped back and studied me for a moment. "I reckon our young'uns what attend school like you well enough and that's good enough for me.

You'll excuse me, though, if I don't bother introducing you to the rest of 'em. It'd be a miracle if you remembered all their names. Even I have a hard time of it." Winking, she burst out laughing and I couldn't help but join in, thinking how much I already liked Thorney's wife.

The day grew warmer as the sun made its arc over the sky but a nice breeze cooled the sweat from my brow as I skimmed the sorghum juice. I liked watching the mule or horse assigned to the task as it moved in a circle around the grinder, producing the power for the mill to grind the cane, squeezing the juice into the vat beneath. And the men and sometimes older boys as they fed the cane into the grinder, careful not to let their sleeves get caught or placing their hands too deep within the mouth. Most of all, I liked watching my husband as he worked stacking the cane and carrying the vat to the evaporator pan, the muscles beneath his shirt moving, the fierce look of concentration on his brow as he went about his chore. From time to time, he would glance at me as if he knew I was watching and we would smile at one another and I thought how happy I was to be here in this time and place with this man and these people.

Vera nudged me, chortling to herself as she whispered, "You're young, Moonfixer, still got that love glow about you. In another six, seven years, the only time you'll be looking at your man will be to tell him to fetch more wood for the cook stove." I smiled at her, thinking, oh, I hope it never comes to that.

During my times away from the boiler pan, I continued to familiarize myself with the other women and men, pairing my school children with their mothers and fathers. I was pleased to meet Charlie and Melanie Davis, parents of my students Mark and his twin brothers Garvin and Marvin. Although Mark was mischievous and fun-loving, these boys were especially dedicated to their studies and I wanted to tell their parents how pleased I was by their progress. As we talked, little Mark darted up, excited that Thorney had told him he could take a turn at feeding cane into the mill. "Just be careful," we all warned him as he ran off, shouting his good news to the other children.

We ate lunch in shifts and I was lucky enough to eat when Fletcher did. We piled our food on plates and found a bed of pine straw beneath a fragrant tree at the edge of the forest. I looked behind me, marveling that we seemed to be right on the edge of night and day – the forest looming dark and mysterious behind us, the yard in front bright and sunny. A shiver swept through me with a sense of great foreboding and I scooted closer to my husband. He smiled at me, not understanding I needed his comfort and warmth. Oh, please, I prayed, don't let anything ruin this beautiful day.

But that was not to be. Mid-afternoon, when they were feeding the last batch of cane through the grinder, as I was taking my turn skimming the boiler pan, I heard a screech so shrill and horrific, gooseflesh broke out on my arms. Men shouted and women screamed as I jerked my eyes up, toward that terrible sound, and saw young Mark, his right arm down the mouth of the grinder, squealing as he struggled to get free. I dropped the paddle, watching as Fletcher rushed over and yanked on the bridle of the mule moving around the grinder, forcing him to stop. Men swarmed over Mark, working to pull him away. And when they did, all that came up from the yaw of that cruel machine was torn cloth and flesh, blood pumping into the air.

As they carried him a short distance away and lay him on the ground, I rushed over to help, untying my apron as I ran, thinking we needed to stop the blood flow or he would surely die. A woman behind me kept screaming and I vaguely wished someone would take her away from here, then thought, if that were my child, I'd be screaming, too. Someone shoved past me – Mark's mother, running to the little boy on the ground. Oh, God, I prayed, please help this family. When I got to Mark and dropped to my knees beside him, his father Charlie sat next to him, laying his head on his lap. Melanie touched her son over his little body, saying, "Oh, my baby, my poor, poor baby," over and over again. The blood pulsing from his arm was steadily slowing down and I knew this was not a good sign.

I glanced around for Fletcher but he was there beside me. "What do I need to do, Bess?" he asked.

"Help me tie the apron around his shoulder. We've got to stop this blood…"

We wrapped the apron around Mark's upper arm, right above where the flesh and bone had been torn away, and pulled tight. His little face was so pale and I tried to remember just how old he was but could not focus on anything except that deathly pallor. If he died, how would I tell the other children in my class that the one most liked would never be coming back to school? The smell of blood was all around me and I ignored it as I worked at staunching the flow.

And when Mark looked up at Charlie and said in a small, tiny voice, "Pap, don't let me die," I choked back a sob.

Charlie, tears streaming down his face, put his rough hand on his little boy's face, saying, "Pap ain't gonna let you die, little Markie. I promise you, boy, you ain't gonna die."

His mother looked at me, a desperate question in her eyes. I couldn't bear to acknowledge he would not live so glanced away, back to the boy, watching my hands turn red with his blood as it drained from his body. Mark's gaze would not leave his Pap's and my respect for this family deepened, watching this. This man loved his children above all. I could see that by the way the child clung to his father's gaze and the father to his son's.

I watched as Mark's eyes lost focus and his face relaxed and the last breath left his mouth, and when it was over could only say, "I'm so sorry, I wish I could have saved him," before giving myself to the grief I felt for a life ended far too soon and the pain it would leave behind. Oh, I knew too well that pain and grief. I still felt it for Greenie, my little brother who drowned in Spring Creek, a young, innocent child who brought light and laugher into the lives of those around him, leaving behind dark days filled with tears and rage.

Melanie's screams rang throughout the mountain while women wept and clung to their children, so sorry for the Davises but so thankful it had not happened to their own. I clutched Fletch's hands and prayed I could do something for them. Charlie gently placed his son's head on the ground and moved to hold his wife close while their twin boys gathered around them, crying and clutching at one another. Eventually, some of the men, at the direction of Reverend Redmon, preacher at Stone Mountain Baptist Church, helped Charlie up. When they urged Melanie to stand, she screamed no and clung to her child, his blood seeping into her clothes and onto her face. When Reverend Redmon assured her she would see her boy later after they tended to him, she allowed him to guide her into Thorney's house. Vera and Thorney solemnly followed and I watched them go, knowing how hard the days ahead would be, telling myself I would do everything I could to help them.

A tall, lanky man with a dark-black beard and black eyes knelt down and picked up little Mark. "We'll take care of him," he said when I looked at him.

I nodded as Fletcher helped me to my feet. I noticed my hands, caked in red blood, then watched as men went about the task of cleaning the grinder and emptying the bloody vat. Fletch, noticing this, said, "Come away, Bessie, that's not for you to see."

He led me to the well and pumped water for me as I washed off the blood. I despaired when I saw it caked beneath my fingernails. "You did everything you could," he said, as if reading my thoughts. "It was too late the second that machine caught him. Thorney should never have let a young'un so small feed the cane."

"But he was so happy about it, Fletcher. You should have seen his face." A face I would never see again, smiling and teasing and running around the school yard. I swiped at my eyes, wishing I had not come to this event.

Those whose molasses had been made began to gather their things and leave. I stayed behind, waiting for Fletcher to help with the grinder while pouring the last of the syrup into jars. The mood was solemn and tense and I felt such guilt that I had not been able to help that sweet boy. I could hear crying from the house and wanted to go inside but did not know if I would be welcome or not. Finally not able to stand it any longer, I stepped onto the porch and knocked on the door. One of Thorney's children, a tall young man with acne scattered across his face, his hair dark and lank, looking much like Vera, opened the door and stared at me. "Might I speak with your parents?" I asked.

Without a word, he opened the door. I stepped into a room laden with deep shadows and imagined the ridge behind did not allow much sunlight to seep into this house. I could hear a woman sobbing from another room and children's high wails, men's low, rumbling voices. Vera came to me at once, clutching my hands. "I am so sorry, Vera," I told her, tears gathering in my eyes. "I wish I could have…"

She pulled me into a hug. "Don't you fret none. You done everything you could, I seen that. You tried to help, that's what counts."

But that did not make me feel better. As with Greenie, I wondered why our God would take such a young, innocent life. "Is there anything I can do for the Davises? Anything they need?"

She shook her head. "I reckon they'll have enough family around to help 'em through. All the rest of us can do is just stand by and let 'em know how much that sweet baby meant to us."

"Would you tell them for me that if they need anything, anything at all, Thorney knows how to find me?"

She nodded then turned away, putting her apron to her eyes.

Fletch stood on the porch, waiting for me. "Let's go home, Bess," he said, his eyes filled with sorrow.

The door behind us flew open and Thorney stood there, an axe in his hand.

Fletch pulled me behind him. "Thorney, what're you doing with that axe?" he said, his voice hard and rough.

But Thorney didn't seem to hear him. He pushed past us, off the porch, and stalked across the yard to the grinder. We watched as he raised it in the air and brought it down on the mill again and again, trying to split it apart. The mill was metal, though, and not so willing to bend to the axe but Thorney managed to dismantle it. Finished, he stood back, his hair in his eyes, a wild look on his face. "Get that cursed thing out of my yard," he yelled, looking around him. "It don't belong here no more."

Men hurried to gather up the pieces and load them in a wagon. Thorney watched until the last bit was gone then turned and went in the house, throwing down the axe before he stepped onto the porch.

I took Fletch's hand as we walked to the wagon. Before he helped me up, I said, "If we ever have a child, Fletch, he will not go near something like that."

"No, he will not," Fletcher said.

We didn't talk much on the way home, but from time to time, Fletcher would reach over and squeeze my hand. My husband was not a loquacious man but I had found that most times, his actions spoke so much more than words ever could.

CHAPTER SEVEN

Fall 1906 – Spring 1907

If that don't get your fire going, your wood's wet.

Every year, it seemed we'd barely gotten the school year off to a good start before it closed down again. I understood the need for the break, the children were needed at home to help with the harvest, but usually found it a bothersome disruption. This year, I welcomed the time away, which began the week following the horrific accident at the molasses making. Little Mark's death dwelt on my mind and I made daily forays to his family home, bringing food and offering sympathy, which brought back memories of Green's death and the dark days that followed. I hoped that by the time school was back in session, my students would have come to terms with the loss of their schoolmate.

But fall seemed determined to draw me out of my melancholy with its colorful display of leaves on the trees, cheerful clumps of purple asters, brilliant yellow wands of Goldenrod and tall spikes of dark pink Joe Pye weed vying for dominance in the fields and along the paths.

I spent the time during the break learning how to milk the cow Fletcher brought home the week before. I had never really done this chore by myself, though I sometimes helped Roy when we were growing up. Ginger was a patient creature and I learned quickly enough, but it took me a while to get the rhythm right. And it seemed my hands stayed cramped for half a day at first, but like the learning, my fingers eventually grew strong enough that it didn't bother me. I would talk to Ginger the whole time, and though she never answered back, it seemed she enjoyed my company well enough.

After school resumed, the time seemed to fly by. December that year started out warm, as if nature was giving us a break before she unleashed the fury of winter on us. In early January, after the Christmas break, she did just that, hurling a massive blizzard that I feared would keep us all at home until spring. Those first two months of 1907 were almost as bad as the winter before Green died in the flash flood. It seemed it was always snowing or icing or sleeting. Whatever kind of cold precipitation Mother Nature had in her arsenal, she gleefully threw them at us that winter.

Every morning, when I arrived at the schoolhouse, my first chore of the day was to get a fire going in the wood burning stove. Some days, it was only a matter of stirring up the coals and tossing on a few logs, but sometimes I had to start from scratch with kindling and matches. As the room started to heat, I would go out to the porch and get the bucket, carrying it to the creek to fill with water. At first I did this as my last chore of the day before I left for home. I soon stopped because on the coldest mornings I'd have to use a rock to break the ice that had formed overnight. Carrying it back to the school, I'd set it on the floor beside the stove to warm. By the time the children began to straggle in, I'd be by the stove with a rag handy, ready to wipe faces and hands if needed.

I had taken to doing this the second week of school when I noted that some of my students looked as if they hadn't had a bath since last summer. I couldn't, of course, bathe them completely but I insisted on clean faces and hands and hoped my tidiness would rub off on them at home. It worked with some, mostly the girls, who seemed to want to please me and worked hard at emulating the way I talked and dressed.

It amazed me, I'd never considered myself a fashion fly, but the girls at Cedar Creek School seemed to think of me as such. It put me in mind of Aunt Belle and I sometimes wished I could bring her in one day and watch as the mouths of my students fell open and their wide eyes all but popped out of their heads at her sense of style and fashion. It would be, I thought, entertaining and educational at the same time.

While I waited for my students to arrive, I would go over my lesson plans for the day and prepare any materials I needed to feed the hungry minds of my students. And most of them were hungry, even starved for knowledge, but even as I fed them, I acknowledged that they returned the favor. I loved seeing their eyes take on that bright glint that let me know they understood what I was teaching. It was a blessing for everyone concerned.

Their morning assignment, one easy enough for even the youngest student to conquer, would be written on the chalkboard when they entered, and they would sit at their desk, working quietly. This was my favorite time of the day, when I could sit just as quietly at my own desk and watch them at their studies. Invariably, one of them would catch me staring and give me a bright grin that made my heart turn over. I often pondered where they would be in ten years and if they would remember their teacher fondly.

I also fed some of them in a more literal manner. Noticing the first week of school that several of the children didn't bring lunch with them or go home to eat, I started making extra biscuits and ham in the morning and packing them in a basket to take with me. At lunch, I would discreetly place the food on the desks of the students who didn't have anything to eat. I don't know if it was my discretion or simply an inbred understanding that life was hard at times, but none of the other students ever made fun of the less fortunate ones.

I continued with the weekly riddles, hoping to teach them to think less literally and to use their young minds in a more creative fashion to solve the problem. They had surprised me with their answers to my first riddle, several of them answering correctly that I had not been given the name Bessie at birth but changed it later in life. The others almost all gave me imaginative answers that, while wrong, delighted me. Each Monday morning, I would write that week's riddle across the top of the chalkboard. More often than not, they figured it out and had several inventive solutions ready for me on Friday morning when I called for their answers.

One morning shortly after the fall break, I wrote: "From house to house he goes, so sure and yet so slight, and whether it rains or snows, he sleeps outside all night." The answer was, of course, a path, but the riddle was one of the harder ones I knew and I hoped to challenge their minds after the awful happenings at Thorney's. Plus, I could use it as a lead in to the Cherokee belief that life doesn't end with death but instead leads to another journey.

I was determined to make a difference in their lives as Miss Julia and the other teachers at Dorland Institute had made in mine.

My students, Lord love them, also had lessons to teach me and often challenged me in unexpected ways.

One cold winter day as I was working with the middle grades, I noticed little Jimmy, a third grader, was spending a lot of time near the woodstove, hunkered down with a history book. The students were allowed to take turns sitting on an upturned log by the stove to get warm. Jimmy, however, had been there for more minutes than he should.

When I walked over to reprimand him, he didn't look up but continued to read with his book at a strange angle.

"Jimmy, you need to stop hogging the warmth and go back to your desk so another student can have their turn."

I shivered at a cold draft and turned to look at what I termed Pete's escape hatch. When I'd told Fletcher about it after my first week of school, he'd brought some spare wood from home and patched the hole for me. Feeling the cold, I thought Slippery Pete might have been able to break through the wood and was back to his hi-jinks. But the hole wasn't there and I wondered where the icy air was coming from.

I checked the door to make sure it hadn't been left ajar, and when I saw it shut tight, turned back to Jimmy, looking up at me with his head tilted like a curious dog. "Oh no, Miss Bessie, I ain't a warmin', I'm a studyin' my lesson by this good light here."

He pointed to the wall, and when I looked, I saw a pale shaft of winter sun lying across the book he held on his lap. The light poured through a crack between two logs, and for a brief moment, my heart refused to let my brain think. Jimmy, not from selfishness but from a desire to learn, had removed the chinking from between the logs so he could study.

In the spring when the weather finally warmed, school closed again for spring planting. I spent the time gathering herbs and planting my own garden, and when school resumed, it was time to do the yearly evaluations.

I started with the youngest, working my way up to the oldest, testing them to gauge how far they'd come in the past seven months. I was delighted to note that most of them had done very well and would be moving up a grade the next year. And my top three students were ready to move onto higher education if they wanted.

In May, the weather was so nice and the children restless to be outside. I decided to take them out every day on short hikes into the woods to teach them what I could about nature. I shared some of Elisi's Cherokee stories; why the cedar tree was created and how it holds the spirits of our ancestors, how the animals brought sickness on man and how the plants decided to offer themselves as cures, and why the mist hangs over the mountains.

On the last day of school for that year, we celebrated with a picnic by the creek. I was feeling rather melancholy that day as the picnic brought on thoughts of my dear Green and that fateful day at Spring Creek when he'd been taken from us by a flash flood.

Shaking it off as best I could, I said, "Who wants to hear the story of how the earth was formed?"

Every single hand shot up as one and I smiled. "This is what the Cherokee believe happened. A long, long time ago before there were people on the earth, all the animals lived up in the sky. They were happy until the sky vault started to get too crowded with so many creatures they hardly had enough room to breathe. Every day, they'd look longingly down at the great earth below but it was covered in water and they knew they couldn't survive if they tried to live there.

"One day, frustrated at being so crowded, the little Water Beetle decided to go down and take a look. She swam around on the surface for a while then took a deep breath and dove way far down to the bottom, gathering mud in her pinchers when she finally got there. Then she started swimming toward the surface but before she got there she ran out of air. Dropping the mud, she paddled desperately toward the light, getting there just before her air gave out completely.

"She was alive but she had dropped the mud. Dreading going back and telling her friends about her failure, she flipped over and floated on her back, looking up at the great sky vault. After a few minutes, she bumped into something. When she turned to look, she saw the mud floating on the surface of the water, and it was growing steadily larger.

"She flew back into the sky and was greeted by all the animals who were watching as the mud continued to grow larger and larger. When it finally stopped growing, the animals decided it would be best to wait for it to dry before they went down so they sent down a bird to look for a dry spot. That bird came back all muddy so they waited and then sent down another bird. That bird, too, returned muddy so they waited some more then sent down another bird.

"Finally, they sent the great-grandfather of all the Buzzards down. Grandfather Buzzard was the strongest of all the birds and he flew for a long way over the mud, looking for a dry spot, but couldn't find one. When he got to what would later become the Cherokee land, he was so tired that his wings dipped down, touching the mud, and when he continued to fly bits of mud dripped from his wingtips to form what we now know as the mountains. When he finally flew back up to the sky, all of Cherokee country was covered with huge mountains and valleys."

I gestured to the mountains in the distance. "That's how the Cherokee say the mountains were formed."

"Is it a fairy tale, Miss Bessie?" Sally asked.

I nodded. "It is, of a sort. It's what we call a legend or a myth, a story that the people passed down from generation to generation. My great-grandmother told it to me."

"It ain't true, everybody knows God made the mountains," Marcus said.

It hit me then that telling the myths of the Cherokee to students whose parents were, for the most part, strict Baptists might not be a good idea. The Baptists, even then, were staunch believers in God and the Bible. The fact I was teaching their children that a water beetle had been responsible for creating the earth would not sit well with people who steadfastly believed in creationism.

"Yes, that's true, Marcus, God did create all things. The Cherokee stories I've been sharing with you have been passed down from the earliest Cherokee to their children and their children's children, legends they at one time believed to be true which have become a part of their culture. That's the beauty of the mind God gave us, He blessed us with the ability to think and reason, but also to dream and imagine."

"I guess, but it still ain't true."

I smiled and ruffled his hair. "It may not be true to you, Marcus, but it is enjoyable and interesting learning how the people who once walked these very mountains thought, don't you agree?"

He only shrugged and I sent up a quick prayer for the both of us. For him, that God would help him to see the whimsy and enjoy it, and for me, that his parents wouldn't come to the school when it opened next year and tell me not to tell their son any more fanciful stories.

I made up my mind right then and there that next year I would teach a detailed lesson on ancient legends and myths. Surely if I taught my students the many different stories passed down not only by the Cherokee but the Greeks and Romans, too, the parents would see it as a learning experience and not as a way to turn their children away from their Baptist beliefs.

CHAPTER EIGHT

Summer 1907

If "ifs" and "buts" were candy and nuts, we'd all have a merry Christmas.

Life went on as it always seems to do and Fletcher and I went on with it. The mountain was an ever-changing delight to me, each season giving me something to be grateful for: the beauty of the wildflowers and the misty green of the budding trees in the spring, the bounty of fresh vegetables and bright flowers in the summer, the harvest of juicy fruits and healing herbs in the fall, and plentiful time to rest during the snowy winter.

And oh, how the world beyond our mountain was changing. The death of a queen, an assassination of a president, moving pictures, and two young men over on the coast of our state took to the air and flew like a bird. It was an amazing time with its fair share of inventions and firsts. Major league baseball had its first championship with the Boston Americans prevailing over the Pittsburgh Pirates. They called it the World Series but I never understood why when only American teams participated. Up in New York, they had a railroad that ran through tunnels completely underground and some company called Maytag invented a wooden tub washing machine that would eventually lead to an electric machine that did all the hard work. I admit, I coveted that last one.

Death wasn't hurting for business either. There were

more than a few conflicts and disasters; the Russo-Japanese war, the Russian Revolution—aptly named Bloody Sunday, the eruption of Mount Pelée, and a devastating plague in India.

Why just in 1906 alone, Finland, a small country in Europe, actually gave women the right to vote; there was a major earthquake way on the other side of the country from us; and President Roosevelt, who had inspired the Teddy Bear a few years back, decided he was going to simplify spelling. I laughed at that one but spent the winter studying Andrew Carnegie's list of simplified spelling words to see if it could help me with my teaching. Turned out the list could have been written by some of my students, they had a way with what I called "creative spelling."

Life on our little farm, however, was just the way I liked it, busy and peaceful at the same time.

In July of 1907, Fletcher brought home another cow to join with Ginger in providing milk and all the things that could be made with it. I named her Prissy Bell because she always acted affronted when I set the stool beside her and began to tug on her teats. She'd turn her head and blink her big brown eyes at me, looking offended and accusatory at the same time. I learned pretty fast not to pat her rump in affection after I was finished because she invariably reacted with an offended kick of her back right hoof which left me staring at the milk pooling on the barn floor.

The barn cats, of course, loved it and even Fletcher's hound dog, Fritz, lapped up his fair share of warm milk before I learned not to pat Miss Prissy on her substantial backside.

The other animals, added a few or even just one at a time, took little of my time. With the chickens, it was only a matter of collecting the eggs and spreading some feed. The pigs were even easier than that since Fletcher did the bulk of the work with them.

The hardest part for me was remembering not to become too attached to them since they would inevitably end up on my stove or in the oven.

My morning chores done, I headed off to school when it

was in session, sometimes walking, other times riding the mare Fletcher had attained with his wily bartering ways, something I often teased him about. I swan, the man could talk a king out of his castle and half his kingdom if he put his mind to it. I'd known him to start the day headed to Old Fort to see someone about a business deal or to pick up some coffee and other staples from the general store and come back late in the afternoon with all kinds of things: wood for a bench to set on the front porch, a bucket of lard and 25 pounds of fresh-milled corn meal, cloth for a new dress for me or a shirt for him, and even, once, with a sled loaded down with pots of flowers he thought I might like to have to "spruce up" the front porch.

It seemed he was always trading for something and many times it was something I didn't even know I wanted before he carried it home.

As I said, life went on and for the most part it went on peaceful with very few bumps until the summer of 1907 which turned out to be an eventful one for us and for two of the families on the mountain. And I, with my gift of foresight, would be right in the middle of all that happened.

The first day after school closed for the year was one of those days I loved most on the mountain, the sun so bright it seemed as if God Himself was beaming down on our little house, swirling His fingers in the creek, setting it to bubbling cheerfully over the rocks, and with a gentle puff of breath blown lovingly through His lips, creating a mild breeze dancing through the newly unfurled leaves on the trees. All of this backed up with the song of the birds giving thanks for the day.

After I finished my morning chores, I decided to take myself out to the front porch to sit on my bench for an hour or so and enjoy a cup of coffee before I set off into the woods to gather herbs and wildflowers. Elisi was always strong with me on days like this and I often found myself carrying on conversations with her in my mind.

That morning, Elisi and I talked of many things, the herbs I was planning to gather, the beauty of the day, and, perhaps because I hoped to find some wild strawberries out on my walk or maybe because Fletcher and I had quarreled that morning before he left to go to Old Fort, I found myself remembering the Cherokee story she'd told me about how strawberries were created.

I could practically hear her voice as I sat on my bench and sipped my coffee.

"Long, long ago when the First Man and First Woman were the only people on earth, they argued one morning and the First Woman was mad enough to walk away. The First Man was mad, too, and so he let her go. But soon, he missed her and decided to go after her. He walked for a full day and by the time the sun went down he could just see her, way far off in the distance. He kept walking all night but so did she and when the Sun came up the next day, she was still far ahead of him. The Sun looked down on him with pity and decided to help so it made huckleberries spring up all around her as she walked. The First Woman ignored them and continued walking so the Sun tried blackberries. These didn't interest the woman either so the Sun decided to create a new fruit. The First Woman kept walking, crushing this new berry beneath her feet so the Sun added a scent to the fruit. It wasn't long before the pleasing smell caught the First Woman's attention and she looked down at the crushed berries. When she bent down and picked one up and held it to her nose she discovered that was the source of the smell. It pleased her so much she tasted it and found it to be juicy and sweet. Looking around, she saw the fruit was all around her. She gathered as much as she could hold and then went back toward her husband thinking that he would like the fruit, too.

"And that was how the First Man and First Woman came to be together again."

I remembered asking Elisi what the fruit was and her smiling at me as she told me, "The berries were red and shaped like a heart..."

And of course, I knew.

"They were strawberries," I said out loud though Elisi, of course, wasn't there. But as always with my great-grandmother, there was a purpose to this story at this particular time. Now all I had to do was figure out which it was, a warning against petty arguing with my husband or a sign to look for the wild strawberries.

Shaking my head, I stood up and went inside, still trying to decide what exactly she was telling me.

She didn't answer but I could hear her laughing in my mind as I continued into the kitchen.

All thoughts of Elisi fled when I noticed the tin of Queen Anne's Lace seeds I'd left on top of the jelly cabinet after taking a few out to chew that morning. I stared at the tin as the strangest feeling came over me.

Something was terribly wrong at the Duttons'.

I ran out on the back porch and rang the bell for Fletcher. Where had he said he was going today? Was it to Old Fort? Or was he planning on working around the farm?

I prayed as I yanked that bell as hard as I could and continued to ring it until I saw Fletcher coming toward me at a dead run from the woods.

He bounded up the steps and grabbed my arms. "What's wrong? Are you hurt?"

When I didn't answer, he shook me and I forced the words out. "I'm sorry, I'm sorry, I didn't mean to scare you but we have to go over to the Duttons' right away."

"What? Why would we have to go to the Duttons'?"

I shook my head. "Something's wrong, bad wrong over there."

"What are you talking about, Bessie?"

"Something awful has happened, Fletcher. I don't know what it is, but I know they need help. We have to go."

Fletcher only stared at me then shook his head. "But Bessie, the Duttons live all the way over to the other side of the mountain. We'd barely get there before dark."

"I know but we have to go, if we don't..."

"Are you imagining ghosts again, Bessie?"

I shivered. How could I convince him of something he couldn't see with his own eyes — something I couldn't see with my own? Still, I knew something was wrong as surely as I knew my own name. Tears threatened but I blinked them away. "It's bad, Fletch, and we have to go. That's all I can tell you, we have to."

Despite my efforts, a tear escaped and tracked its slow way down my cheek.

Fletcher sighed. "Are you sure, Bess?"

I nodded.

"Then I guess I better hitch up the wagon."

Relief poured through me and I threw my arms around him. "Thank you, Fletcher, thank you."

"All right, I'll hitch up the mules and we'll go. Get your shawl, it'll be cool after the sun goes down." He turned away to go to the barn.

I put my hand on his arm, stopping him before he could go down the steps. "Thank you, Fletcher ... for believing me."

He patted my hand. "You've never given me a reason not to," he said and turned to walk to the barn.

We heard the gunshot when we were less than a mile from the Dutton place. Fletcher urged the mules to a trot, and when we arrived, we found Anna, the youngest child, in hysterics while her father held her and her three brothers looked on helplessly.

I jumped out of the wagon before Fletch could bring it to a full stop. Mr. Dutton, tears running down his face, looked at me and shook his head. "She won't stop cryin'. I need to go see to..." He broke off, cleared his throat and then swallowed audibly. "She won't let go."

"Pass her over to me, Mr. Dutton. I'll take care of her. You go do what you need to do."

Reaching up behind his neck, he gently withdrew his daughter's arms. She sobbed and tried to cling to him. I put my hands on her shoulders and it took both of us to turn her into my arms. Mr. Dutton awkwardly patted his daughter on the back before walking away with Fletch.

I held Anna as she cried. Piecing together the story from her mutterings wasn't hard. Her sister Thelma had shot herself because she was carrying and the father refused to marry her. Her mother Martha had found Thelma and in despair had turned the gun on herself. I comforted Anna as best I could, shushing her and telling her it would be all right, her Pa and Fletch would see to it.

When she finally calmed down, I led her into the kitchen and sat her at the table. I filled the kettle with water from the bucket and put it on the stove to heat then looked around, searching for something to make a calming tea.

Martha Dutton, thankfully, kept a good supply of dried herbs and plants and I recognized the oat straw as soon as I saw it in a jar on the windowsill. I'd given Mama oat straw tea to calm her down after Green died.

I was searching for the cups when Anna started to talk.

"She, she found Thelma and, and sent me to fetch Pa and the b-boys. She was fine when I left, Miss Bessie, or I swear I wouldn't never've left her but, but..." She lowered her head to her arms.

I rubbed my hand over her back and let her cry it out. My heart ached for her. I wanted to tell her it would be all right but, of course, it wouldn't be, not for a good while, anyway. I knew what it was to lose your mother and a sibling so close together. And now Anna would have to become the woman of the house. She had her father and three brothers to see to and there was no one else to take her mother's place. I'd been lucky in that respect. I had Elisi until Papa sent her away and I'd had my sister, Loney.

As far as I knew, Anna was the only woman left in this family but maybe there was an aunt or grandmother who could help her.

When the water boiled, I made the tea and set it in front of Anna. Pulling out the chair beside her, I coaxed her to drink it and afterwards led her to her bedroom and urged her to try to take a nap.

She curled up on her side, hugging an old, well-loved doll to her chest, and closed her eyes. It wasn't long before her breathing evened out and I knew she slept. I tiptoed out of the room, closing the door behind me, then went back to the kitchen where Fletch and Mr. Dutton were waiting, carrying the bodies of Thelma and Martha. The Duttons' oldest son, Tom Jr., stood close, his gaze downcast, wringing his hat in his hands.

"Do you have an old quilt, Mr. Dutton, or something else I can cover the table with?"

He only stared at me as if I was speaking in some foreign language he'd never heard before. Tom Jr., spoke up after a few moments. "I'll take care of it, Miss Bessie."

"Thank you." I looked at Fletch. "Where are the other two boys?"

"Tom sent them to tell the neighbors and see if the women can come help."

"Good."

Tom Jr. came back in with a quilt worked in the Wedding Ring pattern. It looked to be fairly new.

"Don't you have an older one?" I asked.

"That was my Martha's favorite. She'd want that one," Mr. Dutton said.

"But I can't promise it won't get stained and ruined."

"Don't matter. She always said she wanted to take it with her when she went."

It seemed to me she would want one of her daughters to have it, and since Anna was the only one left, it might be important for Anna as well since it was her mother's best-loved quilt. But it wasn't for me to say, so I simply helped Tom Jr. spread the brightly colored quilt over the table and then watched as Fletch and Mr. Dutton laid Martha and Thelma side by side on it.

Fletcher put his hand on my shoulder. "We'll be out in the barn working on the coffins, Bessie. The neighbor women should be here in a bit to help, but if you need anything before that, ring the bell and I'll do what I can."

"I should be fine but thank you. Tom Jr., will you bring me your mother's sewing basket, please?"

His face pale, he nodded and went into the other room. Fletch hesitated then reached into his pocket and pulled out two coins. "That's all I have. I'll ask Tom if he has a couple more."

"Fletch?"

He turned to look at me. "Yeah, Bessie?"

"Would you wait and take Tom Jr. with you? He doesn't need to see this."

Tom Jr. came back carrying a large basket overflowing with scraps of material and clothes waiting to be mended. I thanked him as he set it on the floor beside the table.

Fletcher put a hand on his shoulder when he straightened up and looked around helplessly. "Come on out to the barn with me, Tom Jr., we can help your pa."

He went willingly enough.

I knelt down and rummaged through the sewing basket, finding numerous strips and squares of cloth. Taking two of the strips, I tied them around Martha's and Thelma's faces to hold their mouth closed then placed the coins Fletcher had given me over Martha's eyes and covered her face with one of the squares of cloth.

Fletch came back and handed me two more coins, kissed me on the forehead and went out again.

I closed Thelma's eyes and anchored them with the coins, then covered her face with a cloth. I bowed my head and said a prayer for their souls. Grateful the Baptists didn't place the same stigma on suicides that the Catholic Church did, I prayed they would both be delivered into God's waiting hands and made to feel welcome in their new home.

When I opened my eyes, Anna stood in the doorway watching me.

"I want to help, Miss Bessie."

"All right, Anna." I held out my hand to her and she walked over to take it.

"What do I do?"

"We need some water and soap to wash their bodies and when that's done we'll need their best dresses. Why don't you start by heating some water and telling me where your ma kept her rag bin?"

Her bottom lip quivered and I was afraid she wouldn't be able to do this but she breathed in a ragged breath then firmed her mouth and nodded.

"Ma kept a bucket of rags out on the back porch. I'll bring it in and then I'll go to the well and get the water."

It seemed to help her to have something to do, and after Nellie Holt and Mary Penland arrived, I set her to making tea, and when she'd done that, sent her to get her sister's and mother's Sunday dresses.

Nellie and Mary and I worked in silence for the most

part, cleaning the wounds first. They were oddly similar in nature, as if Martha had aimed the gun to pierce her heart in the exact same way it had pierced her daughter's.

Later, after the hated chore was finished, we moved them to Martha's bed. They would rest there until the next day when they'd be placed in the ground at the cemetery of the church the family attended.

I volunteered to remain in the room with the bodies and told Anna to go on to bed. She squared her shoulders, wiped the tears from her eyes and told me she wanted to stay, too. I couldn't object. I remembered not wanting to leave Green or Mama after we'd prepared their bodies for burial.

The neighbors were already arriving, many carrying bowls or platters of food. As they came in to pay their respects, I tried to keep my mind off those hated memories of the deaths I'd attended in Hot Springs. Green, Mama, and finally Druanna, all were in that room with me.

It all seemed so pointless and I wondered if Thelma or Martha had given any thought to the ones they'd left behind. To the pain and agony their family would have to face and how it would affect them. I could understand Thelma's actions but found myself struggling to understand why Martha chose to end her life when she had other children and a husband who needed her.

Later, when I found myself alone in the bedroom with Anna, who cried silently as she sat beside me, I tried to comfort her by telling her what Elisi told me after Druanna's death. "The Cherokee believe when a person dies, it only means their body is dead. But the spirit lives on. Your mama and sister, their spirits are free now and they have begun their next journey together. That should comfort you, Anna, that they'll be together, I mean."

Anna looked at me and shook her head then turned back to the bodies lying side by side on the bed. Her hand shaking, she reached out and stroked her mama's cheek.

I put my arm around her, hugging her tightly to my side. "This is hard, Anna, believe me, I know. I lost my mama and my younger brother when I was a year or two older than you. It's the hardest thing in the world to get through but you have to be strong for your papa and your brothers. You'll be the woman of the house now and they'll be counting on you." I turned her to face me and gripped her shoulders, waiting until she looked at me. "You hang on to your faith in God, and if it helps, you remember what the Cherokee believe. Their spirits are flying free now, nothing else will ever hurt them again, and they'll always be together." I let her go, pulled my handkerchief out of my sleeve and handed it to her. "Maybe it'll be of some comfort to you."

She didn't say anything, only covered her eyes with the handkerchief, but the next day after the ceremony at the church, Anna came up to me and thanked me for telling her about the Cherokee belief that the spirits live on. "Mama and Thelma, they'll, well, maybe they will be all right since they have each other. It does make it a little easier to bear, Miss Bessie. Thank you for telling me. I, I can't say for sure I believe what you said. I think they're in heaven right now, but wherever they are, they're together and that's the important part."

I remembered that when the next death happened, and though it had been a bit of comfort to Anna, I found it harder to swallow when it pertained to one of Fletcher's family.

At least this time when I told him he needed to get to his family's home place right away, he didn't question what I'd said. He didn't even wait for me, instead took the mare and rode as fast as he could to his parents' home at the Elliott homestead in Broad River. I took the time to close the house up and then followed along behind him on foot, Fritz at my heels. It was a long walk but it gave me time to settle my thoughts and come to terms with whichever death would greet me.

Fletcher's father, John Lafayette Elliott, died without warning in his sleep on the night of July 5, 1908, two days before his 60th birthday. Fate's days of being the "best whiskey maker in the county" were over and it hit Fletcher very hard.

Truth be told, it hit me hard, too. I can't say I was ever really close with Pa Elliott, but after living in his house for five years, I had come to love him. He may have made his living selling moonshine, something many considered illegal and more considered a sin, but he was a kind man with a delightful sense of humor who loved nothing more than a good story. We would often sit around the fire on a winter's night and I would tell one of my favorite Papa or Elisi stories, or I would read out loud from one of my books. His favorite: *A Christmas Carol* by Charles Dickens. He would cackle at old Scrooge and his miserly ways, laugh outright at his giddy ramblings when he woke up on Christmas morning a changed man, and though it was hard to tell in the dim light of the kerosene lamps, I often caught a glint of tears in his eyes at the end of the story when Tiny Tim is saved and Scrooge comes to live a long and happy life.

Fate Elliott gave me my nickname and welcomed me sincerely to Old Fort. He was the first person who made me feel as if I might have a place here on this mountain and in the Elliott family. He was, in short, an easy man to love.

Comfort, which had been so easy to give Anna, was a different matter when it came to Fletch. He'd loved his father but disapproved of his lifestyle and often warned him that liquor would kill him in the end. I don't know for sure if it was any solace to the son that his father's death was the result of nothing more than natural causes and that he had died beside his wife of 38 years.

I told Fletcher the same thing I told Anna about the Cherokee belief that the spirit went on but it didn't seem to help. His grief changed him, making him withdraw a little more for a while. He'd always been a quiet man, but in those weeks following the death of his father, he hardly had a word to say to anybody. I was worried he'd never pull out of it and then we got some happy news; my brother Roy and Alice Hill were planning to be married in the fall.

CHAPTER NINE

Summer 1907

Wadn't nothin' between him and the Lord but a smile.

As it turned out, a good bit of my healing business came from Thorney Dalton whom the mountain people nicknamed "White Lighnin". Since the death of Fletcher's pa, Fate, Thorney's moonshining business grew such that he supplied most of the region with brew from his still. He sold it down at Dwight "Hunchback" Smythe's store in Old Fort and rumor had it people from all over the country bought his moonshine. Of course, it wouldn't have surprised any of the mountain folk if Thorney himself had started that rumor. But the revenuers were always after Thorney and he was constantly moving his still, resulting in cuts and lacerations and broken bones from Thorney or one of his 13 children.

Thorney came to see me early one morning, moving with caution, using his rifle as a cane and wincing with each step he took. I was returning from the barn when I noticed him laboring up the path to our house. He spied me and when he drew near, said, "Mornin' Moonfixer. I reckon I'm a needin' your help this morn."

I motioned him inside the kitchen, wondering what he'd done now. "What's wrong, Thorney, you twist your ankle?"

He eased into a chair, grunting with pain, and leaned the rifle against the table. I eyed it, thinking Thorney's rifle was always within arm's distance no matter where he was. The few occasions he attended church, it rested at his feet, and I'd even seen him carry it into the outhouse. Gossip was he took it to bed with him, placing it between himself and his wife. With so many children, I imagined that wasn't the whole truth. Thorney squirmed, trying to get comfortable. "No, ma'am, got me a bad case of the poison ivy, though."

I studied his narrow, fox-like face, brown and creased from the sun; tried to see through his white beard lying tangled down the front of his overalls, covering his cheeks, chin, neck and upper chest; then focused on his hard, calloused hands, the nails grimy with dirt. I couldn't detect a hint of the wicked rash anywhere.

As I searched my herb shelf for sumac, I said, "Well, I sure can't see it so you'll have to tell me where it is." Thorney was quiet so long, I turned around to see if he was still there. I tried not to smile at the blush covering what I could see of his face.

He looked out the door. "I, uh, well, I was,uh, doin' my business, you see, out in the woods up behind my...well, I guess some of that old poison must have got itself tangled in the leaves I used to..."

I nodded and turned back to my search, catching sight of the plant I thought most colorful with its green leaves and burgundy stalks topped with red berries which I occasionally used to make tea. I stripped the stalks of their leaves and berries, and added them to a pot of water, then placed this on the cook stove to boil. I pulled out a chair and sat across from Thorney. "After that boils, we'll need to let it cool down so you may be here awhile. Can I get you something to eat or drink while we wait?"

Thorney shifted in his chair. "No, ma'am, I reckon I'm good enough for now. Just hopin' to get some relief." He gave me an expectant look.

"It should help. Just be sure from now on when you're doing your business in the woods to check the leaves you use before you grab them up."

"I usually do that, I shore enough do, but I was in a bit of a hurry. Seen me a bear close by and didn't want him to get a good whiff of me and think it was dinner time."

I nodded, thinking he was more than likely hiding from revenuers who were always trying to nab him.

Thorney finally got comfortable and looked at me, a twinkle in his eyes. As if catching my thought, he said, "You hear about my roustabout with the revenuers?"

I'd heard rumors but nothing of significance. "Can't say as I have," I answered.

He worked his mouth, looking around the room.

"You need a spittoon?"

"Sure would be nice if I didn't have to get up and down again. It takes awhile to get to where I'm sittin' in the right spot."

I fetched a tin cup off the counter and gave it to him. "Thank you, Miss Bessie." Thorney spit in the cup then carefully leaned back. "Well, I heared from my cousin Otis..." He squinted my way. "You know Otis? He works for the sheriff? Tall, skinny feller with an Adam's apple that takes up most of his neck?"

"No, I don't think so."

Thorney shrugged. "Well, you're still right new to these parts, you'll meet him soon enough, I expect."

I smiled to myself. *Right new.* I'd been on this mountain for years now but suspected it would be many more before the mountain folk truly accepted me as one of their own.

"Round about a couple of weeks ago, Otis told me the revenuers was gonna be payin' me a visit, looking for my still. Now, I got it well hid behind them big rocks on Mule Trot Ridge." He eyed me with suspicion. "I reckon I can trust you not to tell them fellers where my still is."

I shook my head. "And deprive the country of your famous brew? Of course not."

Thorney didn't catch the irony, simply beamed with pride. "I do brew me a mean 'shine, even if I say so myself." He shook his head. "Sure was sorry to see ole Fate go but he did me a big favor when he died. Most of his customers come over to me, and I want you to know, me and my family sure do appreciate the business. Anyway, I didn't have no fear them revenuers'd find it, but just them lookin' for it'd be a hardship on me. I got my old woman and 13 young'uns to feed and that still does well enough at providin' for us all, I reckon. So I figured I needed to find a way to discourage them fellers from comin' back.

"Well, the day they paid me a visit was a hot one, I tell you, and by the time they got to my house from the road – as you yourself know, Miss Bessie, it's a right far piece, a good three miles at least – they was drenched with sweat. I happened to be outside checkin' on my chickens so I just leaned on my rifle and watched them come. When they got to me, the biggest one said, 'Are you Mr. Thorney Dalton?' and I answered I reckoned I was. I could tell from his speech he was some kind of Yankee. I don't cotton to Yankees but them was the feds so I minded my manners. He went on to tell me they had reports of an illegal still and they'd come to destroy it and arrest the operators then asked me if I had any information about such a still. I told him I shore didn't know about no such thing.

"By that time, my old woman, young'uns, and no-count son-in-law Loose Tooth Sawdemeyer had moseyed on down to have a look at them strangers. Livin' so far out of the way, we don't get too many visitors, you know, so it was a special day for us. Now, my young'uns are like me, they don't go nowhere without a weapon of some kind. Why, even my 5-year-old boy carries a knife with him. Them revenuers looked at all of us and their eyes started lookin' shifty. I reckon they was a bit intimidated seeing all them guns and knives pointin' at 'em.

"I proceeded to tell them revenuers I hadn't seen nothin' like that around these parts but I'd sure enough cooperate with 'em and guide 'em through the thickets if they wanted." He gave me a wink. "'Course they didn't know I could take them into places on the back side of Round Mountain it'd take 'em days to get out."

I grinned at this. No one knew these mountains like Thorney Dalton.

"I could tell by the way they was lookin' at me they thought I was the one operating the still but they made one big mistake." He paused.

"What was that, Thorney?"

"They figured me for some dumb ole hillbilly. I might be old and I might be a hillbilly but I ain't dumb, not by a long sight. I fell off that ol' turnip wagon a might long time ago. I could tell by the way they was eyin' me they figured the still might be in one of the places I'd steer 'em clear of, so the big man agreed to let me guide 'em and asked where I thought it might be. I pointed to the rocks on top of Mule Trot Ridge and told 'em they could get a good look at the whole country from up there. Now, as I said, it was a mighty hot day and them revenuers was sweatin' like a preacher in a whorehouse. I told them my well was dried up but I'd take 'em over to Quick Step Springs so they could get some cool water afore we took off a-huntin' the still. You may not know this, Miss Bessie, but anybody who drinks there gets the quickstep runs, that's why it's named that. So I hollered at my two oldest boys to bring their weapons and come with us." Thorney shook his head. "I got 13 young'uns, you know, and don't remember half their names. The old lady kept pumpin' them out real regular until I got old wider Witch Hips Hudgins to fix a mess of poke berry seeds and Joe-Pye weed juice to keep her from having anymore." He eyed me. "You might want to remember that recipe, Miss Bessie, if'n you get any woman don't want no more babies. It must work 'cause the old woman ain't dropped one in two years now."

I nodded my head, making a mental note. I hadn't heard of this concoction.

"Anyhow, me and my sons and the two revenuers went on our way and at the spring me and my boys pretended to drink the water while watchin' them revenuers drink several cups of it. Why them idiots even poured it over their fool heads to cool off."

Thorney waited while I got up to take the boiling pot of sumac off the woodstove. I hoped he'd finish the story before it cooled. Knowing Thorney, this would be a good one.

"So I took 'em on up a trail different from the one I use to get to Mule Trot Ridge, up through some dense laurel and blackberry thickets. Now, me and my boys know how to get through them thickets but them feds got scratched and jabbed the whole way through." He snorted and spit into the cup I had provided. "Damn Yankee revenuers. So we went on down into Rattlesnake Den, that's the name of that small valley over there 'cause it's full of them vile snakes. I figured I'd let the feds lead at that point and it weren't long before we heard them rattlers warnin' them revenuers they better get out of there. Those fellers come runnin' and jumpin' back through a briar patch even a leather-hided mule wouldn't go through." Thorney took a moment to laugh at this vision, me joining in.

"So I proceeded to lead them around the side of the ridge and through another laurel thicket. When we finally got to the top, them revenuers was all scratched up with cuts all over 'em, their uniforms was torn in several places, and they was plumb worn out while me and my boys didn't have a scratch on us. Now my still was right below us but I'd covered it with limbs and briars and they couldn't see too well down there. I told 'em there was a rattlesnake den down there but I'd take them on down if they wanted. They allowed as they was content to look around from up there. I figured they reckoned my still weren't there since I'd so willingly led them to this spot.

"Well, them feds took their time lookin' around and finally the big one pointed to Ghost Holler." He hesitated. "You heared about Ghost Holler?"

"I have but I don't know where it is, Thorney."

"Why, it's over there on Round Mountain, that rocky holler leads up to a stiff rocky cliff. The leader said he'd like to go up that holler and that's exactly where I was wantin' him to go but I put a worried look on my face and told them that was Ghost Holler and I weren't goin' up there cause they was ghosts in it. But that big feller just smiled and said the still was probably there at the cliffs at the upper end of the holler and we was goin' up there and he wanted me to come with him. So we worked our way back down through the dense thickets, but before we got to the gap below the ridge, the other fed began to fidget and squirm and rushed to the side of a large briar bush and pulled down his britches. I told him he could use them shiny leaves beside him to wipe but not to use the other ones 'cause they was poison ivy."

He sighed. "I reckon I'm paying for my prank, Miss Bessie."

I laughed at this. "The Lord works in mysterious ways, Thorney."

He nodded. "Yep, He sure do. Well, it weren't long after that the leader grunted and ran over there and pulled his britches down, too. Sure looked to me like Quick Step Springs is still a-workin' its magic. After that, we worked our way through the brush and briars to the end of the holler, them feds stoppin' several times to squat. I got to admit, them men was pretty tough to keep going after all they'd been through. We entered the holler and I kept lookin' around like I was scared and lookin' for ghosts and told them feds to go on ahead of me. I don't know if you know this, Miss Bessie, but it's called Wasper Hell Holler 'cause they's a large number of them mean wasps that have nests on the bushes and rocks there. Well, soon I heard them feds start cussin' and runnin' through the bushes ahead of us. Me and the boys dropped to the ground and lay still. Them wasps will fly a few feet above the ground huntin' their prey and they was huntin' them feds so they flew right over us.

"After awhile, we made our way down the holler and about a mile down saw them feds sittin' behind a large rock, their faces and hands red and swollen from them wasp stings. I come up to them and said, 'I tole you they was ghosts in that holler. We don't never go up there especially at night.' Dusk was comin' on so I looked up at the sky and told them we'd better get back home afore it gits dark 'cause they's all kinds of varmints runnin' in these woods at night. Told 'em I've seen bears and painters and snakes and wolves there after dark. By that time, them feds was happier than a pig rollin' in mud to give up the search and said they'd start again the next day. I told 'em we didn't have much room in the house with 13 young'uns runnin' around but they was more than welcome to sleep in the barn so back we went.

"When we got to the house, them feds took off running for my two-holer outhouse while me and the boys got two featherbed mattresses and put them in the barn on top of the hay. I forgot to tell them fellers the mattresses was full of hungry bedbugs and the mosquitoes was thick as molasses at night in the barn. Me and my family use the milky juice of the Joe-Pye weed to soothe bites and stings from bedbugs, chiggers, mosquitoes and bees but I didn't bother to tell them feds this. They wouldn't use my hillbilly remedies no ways.

"I guess you can figger them feds didn't get much sleep that night. They was scratched and cut all over and their uniforms was hangin' off 'em in rags. Their behinds was raw from the spring water and the poison ivy blisters and their sensitive places covered with chiggers. Them bedbugs bit all night and the mosquitoes was hungry all right, and being it was too hot to get under covers, they had them a feast. Late in the night I reckon they heard blood-curdlin' yells coming from up in the woods above the barn. It was just a coupla' my boys practicin' their Rebel yells so they could be ready just in case the damn Yankees decide to give us more trouble but them feds didn't know that. I also forgot to them 'em that the early morning sun makes the waspers active around the barn. When I got up and went to the barn the next morning, them feds was long gone back to civilization. Why they didn't even wait to say goodbye."

Thorney and I had a good laugh over that. He might be a mountain man but he was quite the storyteller.

But he wasn't finished. "I saw the sheriff later down at Smythe's Store – that's where I take my moonshine to sell, you know – and he asked me what I did to them feds. He said they was real wild-eyed when they come out of the woods and looked like they'd been runnin' around all night with nothin' between them and God but a smile. He had to take 'em to ol' Doc Widby's place, they was so eaten up by bugs and their eyes was almost swelled shut from the stings. I told Sheriff they weren't too good in the woods, that I told them not to go up Ghost Holler but they wouldn't listen. Told the sheriff he knows what the woods are like at the back side of Round Mountain but them boys just kept lookin' for a still that weren't there."

Thorney spit tobacco juice in the cup and grinned at me, his remaining teeth stained brown. I shook my head. "Thorney Dalton, you are a caution."

The twinkling in his eyes told me he appreciated this.

The tea had cooled by this time so I poured some into a jar. I turned back to Thorney, whose face was now bright red.

"Um, if'n you don't mind, Miss Bessie, I'll be a-puttin' that on my own backside, no need for you to bother with that."

I smiled. "Just pour some over the rash, Thorney. It will ease the itching and should help the blisters to go away."

He got to his feet, leaning on his rifle to help him up, and reached for the jar. "I do thank you, Moonfixer. I tried the Joe-Pye weed but it didn't do much good. I reckon from here on out, I best be more careful about where I choose to..."

"Or more thoughtful about playing pranks, Thorney. You reap what you sow, you know."

"So I've been told, Miss Bessie, so I've been told."

I smiled, watching as he limped out the door and down the pathway to the road. I figured as soon as he was out of sight, Old Thorney would be stepping into the woods to administer the medicine as soon as he could.

CHAPTER TEN

Fall 1907

Old Stomping Grounds.

Later in life, it would be the tunnels I remembered from the long train trip in the late winter of 1901, taking me away from my family and my beloved hometown of Hot Springs to my new life as a married woman in the Broad River Township of North Carolina. There were seven of them, all on the downward slope of Swannanoa Gap as the train chugged its way into Old Fort, all blasted into the mountain as if an angry giant had driven his fist into the unrelenting rock over and over until it gave way, leaving a gaping hole big enough for the train to get through.

Only fancy; I knew, the railroad had been the work of men, most of them convicts, all of them working for little or no wage and even less recognition, but it was a way to keep my mind off what was waiting for me when the train finally stopped.

I grasped Fletcher's hand every time the rock obliterated the sun as we went into the depths of the mountain, apprehension making my hand damp, fearful it might collapse on top of us. Fletcher, as if attuned to my feelings, would squeeze my hand and my grip would relax a bit, a sense of wonder overtaking me as I watched the barely-there light grow ever brighter.

At some point, about midway through I'd say, I would marvel at the seeming impossibility of mere men creating a tunnel in a mountain made up of unyielding stone. How many hours of hard labor had gone into each one and how had they known where the tunnel would come out?

As the light continued to brighten, the wonder gave way to anticipation. What would be on the other end? Would it be more of the never-ending mountain forests or would it be one of the tiny towns bustling with people, crowded with houses and dotted with churches and schools? And whatever lay ahead, would I be lucky enough to catch another glimpse of the manmade geyser which had been constructed in what was to become my new home?

And finally, each time we came back into the sunshine, easing out of the giant's grip, the keen eagerness gave way to excitement and hope, especially when I was treated to the sight of the water spearing up into the heavens.

The geyser itself wasn't a work of nature or even one of God's many feats of glory, but like those seven tunnels, it was a work of man, located in front of the Round Knob Hotel in Old Fort and dedicated to the 120 men who'd lost their lives constructing the railroad and those tunnels through the treacherous stretch of mountain land in the Swannanoa Gap. It was, to my mind, an awe-inspiring sight, albeit tinged with sadness.

Oh, my emotions were everywhere that day, hopping around like a rabbit in springtime, never settling in one place for long. Fascination, excitement, anticipation, and most importantly, hope. Hope that I'd get along with my new in-laws, faith that I'd find a teaching job, and heartfelt desire that my marriage would be happy.

Fletcher and I had been married for only a week and a day but hadn't yet lived together as man and wife except for the first night we'd spent as Aunt Belle's and Uncle Ned's guests at the Mountain Park Hotel in Hot Springs. The next morning, Fletcher had gone to work at the lumber mill and I had returned to my childhood home for the week, hoping I could convince Papa to give us his blessing.

It hadn't worked out that way. Papa stayed away from the house and his family, not even showing up for meals, slinking into the house after everyone had gone to bed.

Thankfully, he showed up at the train depot the morning we left to say goodbye and glare at Fletcher, his way of warning my new husband he'd better take care of me or he'd have to answer to Papa. We'd hugged and assured each other of our love and then it was time to go. I'd stood on the platform of the caboose, waving until I couldn't see him anymore.

As we neared the town of Old Fort, all of my jumping emotions fused into a mass of anxiety that settled in my stomach like a wet, clammy boulder. Despite my wet palms, I clutched Fletcher's hand in mine and wondered where in the devil I'd left my gloves. Aunt Belle would be horrified but then I didn't have to worry too much about my prim and proper aunt this far away from home.

And now we were heading away from Old Fort and back to Hot Springs and home had an entirely different meaning to me. I sighed as I realized I missed my home even as the train took me toward the town I had once loved so ardently and the family I hadn't seen in over six years. I had missed them, sure, but I loved my new life on Stone Mountain in the small house with the creek running through the front and the beautiful cantilevered barn built by my husband and our friends.

I looked forward to seeing my family again, especially my brothers and sisters. Papa, well, I admit to feeling a bit anxious about Papa. He hadn't approved of my marriage and I wondered how he would react to having Fletcher staying in the house with him.

I shoved the thought and unthinkingly clasped Fletcher's hand in mine as the train entered a tunnel.

There was nothing I could do about Papa. All the worry in the world wouldn't change how he would act with my husband. The only thing I could control was how I reacted to his actions. My heart belonged with my husband now. I was no longer a little girl hanging on her father's every word and agreeing with him no matter what. Hadn't I proved that when I married Fletch against Papa's wishes and moved with him to Broad River Township?

I squared my shoulders. Yes, I had and there was no going back. I was happy with my husband, pleased, even proud of the life we'd carved out for ourselves on Stone Mountain, delighted with the new friends I'd made, and downright fulfilled in my job as a teacher at Cedar Grove School.

As we emerged into the sunlight once again, Fletcher squeezed my hand. "We made it through another one, Bessie-girl."

I squeezed back and turned my mind to happier thoughts, determined to enjoy this trip. "Won't be long until we're in Asheville again. I wonder what we'll see this time?"

He laughed. "Whatever it is, I'll bet its worth seeing. Maybe if we have time we'll take us a ride in one of them horseless buggies they have running around."

I shook my head. "The train's enough for me. I don't know that I'd trust those contraptions to take me where I want to go. I'd rather walk anyway. You can see more of the world that way."

"You surely can."

I took my hand away and rubbed it on my skirt and Fletcher once again surprised me with the way he seemed to always know my thoughts. "Don't be nervous, Bess, we'll be all right. Your papa may not think so but I have faith in us, faith that God knew what He was doing when He sent me to work on your uncle's farm."

That shocked me even more. Like Papa, Fletcher had a distinct faith in God, but he didn't often voice his feelings or beliefs, even to me.

I leaned my head on his shoulder, watching the trees whoosh by in a blur of green lightly tinged with fall's colors of gold, red and orange outside the train's window, secure in the knowledge that Fletcher and I both had the faith required to ensure we would always and forever be together just as God wanted us to be.

As the mountain people were fond of saying, God works in mysterious ways, and to me, our marriage was living proof of that. Of course, some might say my determination had swayed God's hand a bit, but I hadn't forced Fletcher to propose or even to court me. True, I may have instigated the whole courtship when I chose him to give me a kiss after finding the red ear of corn at Mr. Dunlap's corn shucking and after a few dances demanded he tell me what his true feelings for me were. When he told me he thought he wasn't good enough for me, I'd told him that wasn't his decision to make, but mine, and since I liked him and wanted to be with him, what did he suggest we do about that?

So yes, I guess you could say I carried some responsibility for us being together but I'd felt, and still did, I'd done what was needed to get Fletcher past his shyness and his ill-gotten notion that he wasn't good enough for me.

I sighed again and when he leaned his head against the top of mine, said, "I have faith in us, too, Fletcher. We may not be rich but we have our own home and 400 acres to keep us busy and I am confident that we'll live a long and happy life on our little farm."

"I promise I'll do my best, Bess."

"You already are, Fletcher." I raised my head and looked at him. "I don't care about being rich, really, but the fact that we're both willing to work for whatever we may want or need means a lot. And having the man I love by my side makes it mean that much more."

He took my hand. "You're a strong woman, Bess."

I smiled. "I am that."

He chuckled. "I want you to be happy."

"Teaching makes me happy, helping earn the money to buy our own place makes me happy, tending to the sick people who come to me for help makes me happy, and being Mrs. Fletcher Elliott makes me the happiest of all."

"And one day, maybe our children will make you happy, too."

I nodded. "Yes, that would make me happy, too, but Fletcher..." I hesitated. I didn't know how he would feel about my reluctance to have children until I had taught a few more years and we'd established our lives a little more.

"What is it, Bess?"

"Well, I'm happy the way we are right now. The babies can wait, we have plenty of time."

He turned and looked at me. "Do you want children, Bessie? I don't think we've ever talked about that before."

"I do, one day. I'm not ready to give up teaching yet and I'm really not ready for children yet, either. I suppose people are beginning to wonder when we'll start a family—"

"I don't care about them, Bess," he interrupted.

"No, I know you don't and I don't either, really, but you know how people on the mountain talk. I'm sure we've been the subject of quite a few dinner-table conversations. Not that I'm worried about that. Let them think what they want, there's nothing you or I can do to change that. But like I said, I'm not ready yet. I want to give all my attention to teaching and our farm for a few more years." I squeezed his hand. "I hope you understand."

"All right, if that's what you want." He raised my hand to his lips and kissed the knuckles. "You're a pure-d puzzle to me sometime, Bess. The way you are with those young'uns at school, anybody would think you wanted a dozen of your own." He shook his head. "I can look at you and know I can't live without you even as I know I'll never completely figure you out."

I laughed. "I'm not so hard to figure out, Fletch, I'm nothing more than a young woman in love with her husband and looking to the future."

The train moved into another tunnel and Fletcher took advantage of the sudden darkness to lean over and kiss me while no one could see. "You're like one of those riddles you like to use with your students, Bess. I ain't got the answer yet but I'm looking forward to solving it over the next fifty or so years."

The sunlight beamed down on us once again, and I did a little beaming of my own as I watched the trees flash by. My husband might not say it but he always let me know he loved me in the sweetest ways.

Papa wasn't at the station when the train pulled into Hot Springs, but Roy, holding Thee's hand, and Loney, holding Jack's hand, were all there to greet us. Laughing, Loney and I fell into each other's arms as if it had been centuries since we'd been together rather than a little over six years, both talking at once, joyous in our reunion.

When we finally turned each other loose, I took my time hugging everybody else at least once. Fletcher kissed Loney's cheek, shook Roy's and Thee's hands and then turned to Jack, hiding behind Loney. He winked at her which made her bury her face in Loney's skirts.

I bent down to her and said, "You've grown into a lovely young lady, Jack. What grade are you in now?"

She looked down at the ground and didn't answer.

Loney laughed. "She's a shy little thing but she's doing well in school. Miss Julia says she's ahead of her class, and if she keeps doing well, they might move her up two years this fall. Roy, you help Fletcher with the luggage. We'll meet you at the wagon."

I smiled and hooked my arm through hers. "I don't believe I've ever heard anyone refer to a Daniels as shy. Wonder where she got that from?"

Before she could answer, Thee ran up and blurted, "I got me a dog, Bessie."

I smiled at my little brother, now twelve, who had lost all his baby fat and was beginning to show signs of the man he would become. With dark hair and eyes and a slim, wiry build, I thought he looked to be a smaller version of Papa. "You do?"

He fell into step beside us and regaled me with the tale of Papa and the dog he'd brought home a few weeks ago. "Papa said I could name him. Wanta know what I named him?"

"Of course I do, else how will I know what to call him?"

Thee beamed. "Noah."

I laughed. "That's a strange name for a dog."

"Nope, I call him Noah because when Papa brought him home he was soaking wet and looked like he'd been caught in a flood."

That brought memories of Green's death and I had to force myself to smile. "That's a good name then, Thee."

I looked at Loney and she shook her head. "He doesn't remember and I can't bring myself to tell him," she whispered in my ear.

"It's better that you don't. He'll have plenty of time to

learn about his brother and how he died," I whispered back.

Thee ran off, bored with his sisters' whispering, shouting for Roy to wait for him.

"That's what I thought." Loney smiled. "Well, Bessie, I must say marriage seems to agree with you. You're looking well. Are you happy?"

"More than I ever thought I could be. Fletcher and I are fixing up the house and he keeps busy farming tobacco and cutting lumber that he sells in Old Fort. Did I tell you, I named it Cedar Creek Farm? Of course, I must have in one of my letters. Cedar Creek is the name of the creek that runs in front of the house. But then, I probably wrote you that, too." Laughing at myself, I chose another subject to gush about. "I love teaching and hope to continue with that for at least a few more years. My students this last year all did well and will progress a grade next year." I waved that away. "Well, you know all that since it was in my letters." I stopped, decided to just come out and ask. "Loney, where's Papa? I thought he'd be here to meet us."

"He's in Marshall. There was a ruckus out in Tiger Town last night and he and Mr. Norton arrested three men. They had to take them into Marshall this morning."

"Will he be back?"

"Of course he will. He told me this morning he'd try to make it back before your train arrived but he'd be home for supper no matter what."

"Good. He's...he's not still mad at me, is he?"

"About what? Oh, you mean because you got married and left? I don't think he was ever really mad at you, Bess, he was more troubled or maybe dismayed, you might say. When he sees you and how happy you look, I think he'll be all right." She smiled as she rubbed her hand over my back. "You are happy, aren't you, Bessie?"

I smiled. "As happy as a dead pig in sunshine."

She laughed. "Oh, Bess, you'll never guess, Papa asked me to change the bed linens on his and Mama's bed so you and Fletcher could sleep there while you're here."

That took me aback. "He did?"

"Yes, he sure did."

Hope bloomed in my chest. "Do you think that means he's accepted Fletcher, that he's accepted our marriage?"

"If not, I think it means he's on his way to accepting it, wouldn't you say? I mean, I never would've thought he'd offer that but he did and I think you should take that as a sign he's at least trying."

"Yes, I will."

"And don't tell him I told you this, but he has a surprise for you."

I was so flummoxed by Papa's generosity I couldn't even begin to think what the surprise would be. "I won't, I promise. I can't imagine what it could be."

"Don't try because you'll never guess in a thousand years."

"All right, I won't." A surprise for me? Maybe that meant Papa was, as Loney said, trying to acknowledge my marriage, I said a silent prayer that it also meant he was trying to accept Fletcher as well. "How is Elisi, Loney? I was hoping she'd be with y'all at the train station."

"Oh, Bess, I forgot to tell you she asked if you'd come visit her this week."

At my questioning gaze, she went on. "Elisi keeps to her cabin most of the time. She says traveling is too hard on her."

Alarm skittered up my spine. "Is she sick?"

Loney shook her head. "Just elderly. She's aged a lot since you left but then she's nearing 90 so her frailty is to be expected."

"I'll go see her tomorrow if I can." It warmed my heart when Jack scooted up beside me, shyly placing her hand in mine. I smiled down at her. She still looked like Papa, although she'd never have his height or his burly build. Small and dainty, that was our Jack, with curly dark brown hair and lovely brown eyes to match.

"So, Jackie-girl, is it a mystery for me to figure out or are you going to tell me what grade you're in?"

I listened to Jack's chatter until Loney stopped beside a strange wagon. "Papa had to take ours to Marshall with the prisoners so Roy borrowed Mr. Dunlap's to take y'all home."

She helped Jack into the back where someone, probably Roy, had spread a generous amount of hay. "Thee, hop on up here. We're going to take Bessie and Fletcher home with us and," she winked at him, "we may never let them leave again."

I laughed. "How is Mr. Dunlap? Oh, and Miss Cordy and her Little Bit?"

"They're all fine, looking forward to visiting with you and Fletcher while you're here. I imagine we'll have a steady stream of people in and out of the house for the next week."

"That will be nice." I turned to look for Fletcher. He and Roy had dropped behind as we walked. They now had their heads canted toward each other, talking about something. I nodded in their direction. "Thick as thieves, those two are, I wonder what they're up to?"

"Who knows? Roy's always got something going on these days. Did I write you that he and Alice are thinking about moving to Knoxville after they're married? Roy hopes to get a position with the railroad, and if he does, they can travel to Hot Springs as often as they want. I'll miss them, though."

"Miss cleaning up after him, you mean?"

"No, I won't miss that." She shook her head. "He's always been able to make a mess wherever he is. Once he and Alice are married, that will be her job. Thank goodness." Loney sent a frown in Roy's direction. "I had almost lost hope for him and Alice."

"What do you mean?"

"Well, you know our brother, stubborn as two mules. It took him a while to admit he wanted to marry her. Everybody else saw it before he did what with the way he moped around when Alice was in Knoxville visiting her family. I swan, I wanted to take his prized baseball bat to his backside more times than I could count. Or use it to knock some sense into that thick head of his. I wish Alice luck with him. She's going to need it."

"Oh, Loney, he's not that bad. A little moody sometimes, but all in all, he's a good brother."

"Yes, he is, all things considered. He'll probably make a

fine husband, too, but that will be mainly due to Alice. She handles him better than anybody. Here, hop on up there and let's go home."

Fletcher helped me into the back of the wagon where I sat in the hay. Jack and Thee immediately scooted over to sit on either side of me. Fletcher helped Loney up and she sat down across from me. I let her get settled before I asked, "What about you, Loney? What's going on in your life?"

She shrugged. "I'm still working at the Mountain Park Hotel and for now it suits me but it isn't something I want to spend the rest of my life doing. And I'm still playing the piano at church and the reverend asked me to sit in on the choir practices, too. Seems Sari Bearing—you remember her, don't you, Bess, the oldest of the Bearing sisters?"

I nodded and had to suppress a smile at the thought of Tommy Bearing and the way his sisters were once fixated on seeing me married to their spoiled brother. Thankfully, I'd avoided that and held out for the real man I wanted.

"Like I wrote you, she took over playing the piano after you left but Preacher Linton asked me if I would do it since Miss Sari is getting on in years and is getting a little hard of hearing."

"Yes, Loney, but what about marriage? Any prospects?"

She shrugged. "I've walked out with a couple of boys but so far nothing's taken."

I leaned over and kissed her cheek. "Don't rush it, you've got plenty of time and who says you have to be married anyway? There are some women who never marry and lead full, happy lives. Why there are some who are even talking about getting the vote and running for political office. Who knows what you can do until you try?"

"Yes, I know, the world is changing, but all I really want, Bessie, is a husband and maybe a few babies. I'm not like those forward-thinking women who say we can have a career if we choose." She sighed. "Truth is, all I really fancy is a family of my own."

I might not have wished for the same thing but I understood it as I'm sure most women of the time did. There weren't many options for a woman in the early 20th century except marriage and babies. I wanted that, too, but in due time. I also hoped for so much more although right then I couldn't have told you what that "more" was.

Fletcher, standing a few feet back from the wagon, still talking to Roy, looked up at me and smiled. "All set, Bess?"

Beside me, Loney sighed, then as Fletcher moved to get in the wagon beside Roy, whispered in my ear, "That's what I want, Bessie."

"What?"

"A man to look at me the way Fletcher looks at you, his eyes all full of love. That's what I'm looking for. You're so lucky to have found it."

I squeezed her hand. "You'll find it too, Loney. Just give it time."

"I sure hope so."

Roy drove us home where we found Papa waiting on the front porch. I scrambled out of the wagon as soon as it slowed, racing into Papa's open arms.

"There's my girl," he said as he hugged me tight. "There she is."

I kissed his cheek, laughing when his handlebar moustache tickled, and all I could choke out past the tears backing up in my throat, was, "Papa, Papa."

"Well, now," he said, taking my arms and moving me back so he could see me. "Let's get a look at you, Bessie-girl." His eyes took me in from head to toe and he nodded before pulling me back into his arms. "Damn, Bess, you're a sight for sore eyes. I've missed you girl."

"I've missed you too, Papa," I whispered and let the tears fall.

"Here now, we'll have none of that." He shifted me to the side but kept his arm around my shoulders. Holding out his right hand, he said, "Fletcher."

"Mr. Daniels, it's good to see you, sir."

Papa nodded. "Well, Bessie, let's go in and get you settled and then we'll have us a feast on that ham that's been teasing my taste buds since I got back from Marshall."

Keeping his arm around me, he led the way up the porch steps and into the house. I stopped a few steps in and just breathed, taking in the familiar scent of cedar. I looked over my shoulder at the door and saw the fresh sprigs of cedar spread across the top of the jamb. When I looked at Loney, she smiled.

"I remembered the way you used to do that. It seemed the way to welcome you home, Bess—even if I never knew why you did it." She grinned.

"Elisi..." I cleared my throat. "Elisi taught me to do that. The Cherokee people believe it protects the house and those in it. Thank you, Loney, it really does make me feel welcome."

CHAPTER ELEVEN

Fall 1907

Busier than a one-eyed cat watchin' two rat holes.

That night, Papa gave me the surprise Loney spoke of, a locket he gave Mama shortly after they married. When I pressed the clasp holding its heart shape together, it opened to reveal a small picture of Mama on one side and Papa on the other. I vaguely remembered Mama wearing it before we moved to Hot Springs but after that she'd put it away for some reason. I wondered if it was because of the two miscarriages she'd suffered after having Loney before Papa decided it was time for a fresh start.

Tears formed in my eyes as I smiled at my father. "Thank you, Papa, I'll treasure this all my life."

He took the necklace from my hands and fastened it around my neck before drawing me into a hug. "Your mama always said she wanted you to have it, Bessie. I just couldn't bring myself to give it up till now." As our eyes met, I could see my own pain reflected in my father's and thought how lucky Mama was to have a husband who loved her as he had.

The next day after breakfast, Fletcher and Roy hooked up the mules to Papa's wagon and headed out. They wouldn't tell me where they were going, only that they'd be back late in the afternoon and that I should not make any plans for the next day.

I watched as they pulled out of the yard, my brow creased with puzzlement. Where in the world could they be going and why wouldn't they tell me? I liked surprises as much as the next person, but really, enough was enough. There was, to my way of thinking, too much of a good thing.

"Yoo-hoo, Vashti Lee."

I turned and watched Aunt Belle mince her way down the street. I bit the inside of my cheek to keep from laughing. Aunt Belle, as always, was dressed to the nines in the latest fashion, right down to the kidskin gloves covering her dainty hands. Wearing a full skirt and matching jacket in a material of tiny checks with a velvet collar, she was, without a doubt, a sight to see. The skirt even had a slight train in the back that stirred up a small cloud of dust in her wake. She wore a wide brimmed hat decorated with lace and flowers and tilted low over her forehead. I had no idea how she could stand to wear so many clothes when Hot Springs was in the sweaty clutch of an Indian summer with temperatures that felt more like the dog days of August than October. It was, in my mind, a miracle she didn't melt into a puddle at my feet or at least swoon under the beaming sun after walking up the slight incline to our house.

"Aunt Belle!" I smiled as I opened the gate and walked out to meet her. As she bundled me in her arms, I caught the familiar scent of vanilla and spearmint. "Oh, Aunt Belle, it's so nice to see you," I muttered into her shoulder.

She tightened her arms around me for a few seconds, letting me know she was glad to see me, too, before she released me and stepped back. "Let me have a look at you, girl." Her eyes traveled over me and she nodded. "Well, married life doesn't seem to have hurt you." She speared a look at my midsection but refrained from commenting on the fact I wasn't carrying yet. I could only breathe a sigh of relief that her proper manners would never allow her to speak of anything so crass out in the middle of the street—and I hoped they would keep her from commenting on it after we got inside.

Except if she asked, that would open the door for me to question why she never had children. Was it by choice or chance? Had she distilled one of the herbal concoctions Elisi had taught me would keep a woman from conceiving? Or one of the ones that would end the pregnancy almost before it got started? Or had she been trying for all the many years she and Uncle Ned had been married, only to be met with disappointment every month? My heart told me the latter was the answer and I had to wonder if that was it, was it to be the same for me?

Feeling an unexpected bond with this aunt I'd often ridiculed and laughed at was an unnatural feeling so I took her hand and led her up on the porch. "I was just about to make some tea, Aunt Belle. Would you like some?"

She smiled and I knew I'd hit on the proper etiquette. "Yes, dear." She fanned her hand in front of her face. "I swan, I didn't think I'd make it up that hill in this heat."

"Well, I'm awful glad you did. Come inside and you can rest in the parlor while I make the tea. Loney's back in the kitchen. I'm sure she'll be happy to join us."

I pulled her inside and settled her on the sofa. "I won't be but a minute and I think Loney has some of Mama's molasses cookies hidden away where the little ones can't get to them. We'll have some of those, too."

Her eyes went soft at the mention of Mama, her beloved sister and best friend, and she reached for my hand. "Do you miss her, Vashti?"

I nodded. "I do, Aunt Belle, every day. I just wish I had..." I shook my head, not knowing exactly how to say that I'd never appreciated Mama while she was alive. It was my biggest regret.

Aunt Belle squeezed my hand. "She loved all of you, more than her life. And she knew you loved her, too. Why, Lucinda would be pleased as punch to see you married and happy. You are happy, aren't you?"

I squeezed back. "I am, Aunt Belle, I truly am."

She blinked back tears and her lips curved in a smile. "That's good, then. Now, shoo." She waved her hand, "Go on and get that tea and we'll sit here and gossip like Lucinda and I used to do. I can't tell you how much I miss that."

I turned and went to the kitchen where Loney was finishing up the breakfast dishes. "Oh, Loney, I was going to help with those."

"All finished. Was that Aunt Belle's trill I heard out the window?"

"Yes, she's in the parlor and wants her tea and she wants..." Tears flooded my eyes and I couldn't keep them from falling. "I'm sorry, Loney, I miss Mama so much sometimes."

Loney rushed over and wrapped me in her arms. "Oh, Bess, it's all right. Don't you think Mama would be happy to see you and Aunt Belle carrying on where she left off?"

When I didn't answer, she went on, "Mama wouldn't want us to be unhappy and she'd expect us to carry on in her stead. Right now, that means entertaining Aunt Belle and sharing a few minutes of gossip with her. It'll make her happy, too."

I sniffed then took the handkerchief Loney held out to me.

"Don't you think Mama's looking down from Heaven right now, Bess, and smiling at us? I'm sure she wants to hear all the latest gossip, too."

I smiled and closed my hand around the locket I wore. "You're such a sweet person, Loney, and yes, I do think Mama's smiling down at us and she's very proud of her middle daughter."

Loney blushed. She'd never been comfortable with compliments. "Well, I don't know about that last, but I know what she'd expect of us so we'll spend an hour or so with Aunt Belle, drink some tea and eat some of Mama's molasses cookies."

And that's exactly what we did. By the time Aunt Belle left three hours later to, as she said, "dash home before my husband decides I've run off with the undertaker," I knew everything that had happened in Hot Springs since the day I'd boarded the train for Old Fort: the weddings, funerals, quilting bees, who found the red ear of corn at every one of Mr. Dunlap's annual corn-shuckings and who they asked for a kiss, who was doing something they shouldn't be doing, and who was spooning whom.

After we walked her to the door and followed her out on the front porch, I looped my arm around Loney's waist and we watched Aunt Belle as she strolled down the hill this time, the train on her skirt sending up little poofs of dust as she went.

I gave Loney a squeeze before stepping away. "If you don't need me this afternoon, I think I'll go see Elisi."

Loney smiled at me. "I figured you would."

As I saddled Papa's red mare Bob, a prickle of excitement raced up my spine at the prospect of visiting my great-grandmother. Sometimes I felt I missed her most of all, this wise, elderly woman who taught me much through sage advice and the Cherokee legends she relayed.

By horse, it didn't take long to arrive at Elisi's small log cabin, situated deep in the forest beside the shallow French Broad River. I found her outside her cabin, walking stick in hand, as if she were waiting on someone. She smiled when she saw me.

I hugged her long and hard. "I've missed you so much, Elisi."

She stepped back, a look of happiness on her face. "I have missed my granddaughter too. I enjoy your letters but it isn't the same as being with you."

"I feel that way, too." I glanced at the walking stick. "Are you gathering?"

Her eyes glittered with merriment. "I thought we'd walk among the trees and look for herbs."

So she had known I was coming. I smiled and in answer took her hand and we strolled into the forest, the air becoming cooler as we moved deeper into the woods. Elisi would stop from time to time to study this or that plant, often asking me the name and its medicinal use. At one point, she arched her eyebrows at me. "My granddaughter has not forgotten."

"I use them as you do, Elisi. You taught me well."

I darted glances at my great-grandmother as we walked, noting how frail and delicate she now seemed. Although her hair remained dark, deep grooves had taken hold in her face and her skin looked paper-thin and creased. She moved slowly and carefully and needed to stop often to rest. I had to bite back tears, as a feeling stole over me, strong and sure, I would never see my great-grandmother after I left Hot Springs.

Sensing my scrutiny, she gave me a wry smile. "Age is not kind to the People, granddaughter. Many times I long for the days when my body was firm and agile, but as with all things the Creator has made it that our bodies wither and eventually die." Seeing my expression, she said, "Oh, do not be sad, child, I will live on in spirit and will always be with you."

I swiped at my eyes. "I can't stand the thought of losing you, Elisi."

"You will not. I will be walking with you even though you will not see me."

A flock of wild turkeys came waddling toward us and upon seeing Elisi and me scattered with frightened gobbles. Elisi took my hand and said the words that were my favorite, "I will tell you a story."

"I had hoped for such."

"A story about why the turkey gobbles. In the old days, Grouse had a good voice but Turkey had none. Turkey asked Grouse to teach him to speak but Grouse wanted pay so Turkey promised feathers for a collar and that is how the Grouse got his collar of turkey feathers. Grouse began to teach Turkey and finally said, 'You must try your voice and halloo.' When Turkey agreed, Grouse told him he would stand on a hollow log and when he tapped on it, Turkey must halloo as loudly as he could. So Grouse climbed on the log and started to tap on it, but when he did, Turkey became so excited that when he opened his mouth, he only said, 'Gobble, gobble, gobble.' And that, granddaughter, is why the Turkey gobbles whenever he hears a noise."

I laughed. "I love your stories, Elisi."

She nodded. "You must remember to pass them on, child. Do not let the legends of my people die with me."

I squeezed her hand. "I promise I won't, Elisi."

The afternoon passed quickly and when the air began to cool and the sun seemed not so bright, I took my leave of my great-grandmother, promising to come back before Fletcher and I left. And as I rode home, it occurred to me, she had not asked about my husband or our marriage. But the gift had passed to me from Elisi and I supposed she did not need to.

Back home, I helped Loney prepare supper but Fletcher and Roy still weren't back by the time we ate. It was after dark when my husband and brother finally did return, both of them sweaty and covered in dirt. I met them in the barn, curious about where they had been for so long and what they had been doing all day.

"It's a surprise, Bessie," was all Roy would say as Fletcher just smiled at me and shook his head.

I caught Fletcher's arm as he unharnessed the mules. "Does Papa know?" I demanded.

"Nope, nobody knows except me and your brother. And the only reason he knows is I needed his help. Watch out, now, I need to get this mule brushed down."

I huffed out a breath and stomped back to the front porch where Papa and Loney were sitting.

"What's got your feathers ruffled, girl?" Papa asked.

I plopped down on the steps, crossed my arms and glared at Papa. "Did you ever keep secrets from Mama?"

Papa stroked his handlebar moustache. "Well, now, depends on what you mean by secrets."

I scowled. "What does that mean? A secret's a secret no matter how you look at it."

"Nope, not rightly so. There are some things a woman doesn't need to know about her husband just like there are some things a man doesn't need to know about his wife." Papa chuckled. "And before you ask me what things, I can't answer."

"Won't answer, you mean."

"Yep. If I didn't even tell your mama, why would I want to tell anyone else, especially my daughter?"

"Oh, Papa, stop talking in riddles."

He grinned. "Let me ask you this, and I want you to think hard before you answer. Have you told Fletcher Elliott everything there is to know about you?"

I opened my mouth to say yes but then Papa pointed at me and narrowed his eyes. I thought again and could feel the blush staining my cheeks. There were some things I'd never told Fletcher about myself, some things were too private to share with anyone, even your husband.

I stewed most of the night, not saying much, and when Fletcher and I went to bed, I still wasn't over my snit.

I finally fell asleep long after the moon rose but slept fitfully and was up before the sun the next morning. I washed and dressed quickly then tiptoed down to the kitchen to make coffee and get breakfast started. Papa was already there.

"Good morning, Papa."

"Morning, Bessie-girl." His eyes studied my face. "Looks like someone didn't get a good night's sleep."

I shook my head. "Too many things on my mind." I hesitated for a second. "Papa..." I shook my head again, reached up to get a coffee cup.

"Well, what is it, girl?"

"Nothing. Did you sleep well, Papa?"

"Slept better than you did, I reckon, but I had a few things on my mind, too."

"What things?"

He stroked his moustache and narrowed his eyes at me. "Bess, uh, damn, girl, are you happy?"

"Yes, Papa, I am."

He nodded. "Good, that's good."

"You don't believe that, do you, Papa?"

He shook his head. "If you say you're happy, then I reckon I have to believe it. You never lied to me before." He grinned. "At least, not that I know of."

"No, I didn't and I'm not lying now. I don't expect you to understand, Papa, but Fletcher is my husband and I married him because I love him just as you loved Mama. Fletch and I may not have much yet, but he makes me happy."

"Why?"

"Why?" I drew in a breath, let it out slow. "I don't know how to explain it, Papa, it's a feeling I get whenever I'm with him, a sort of lightness in my heart and a, a rightness in my brain. I'm comfortable with him, even when I'm mad as a hornet at him for something—which hasn't happened much, now that I think of it. He makes me laugh, he makes me feel safe, and he makes me feel loved. He understands me," I looked in Papa's eyes, "even when I do keep secrets from him. Not that there's that many to keep. I haven't exactly lived a life of adventure or done much that needs to be kept secret from anybody. I just, well, I love him, Papa, and that's the only thing that counts."

He stroked his moustache again and I knew I had a ways to go to convince him. "Damn, Bess, he wasn't what I wanted for you at all. He's rough and country and he can't give you the things you need." Looking down at the table, he mumbled, "And he's a damn Republican."

Laughing, I laid my hand on his. "Politics aside, Papa, what you mean is he can't give me the things *you* think I need. Fletcher may not be the man you envisioned me marrying, but he's the man I want and that should be good enough for you."

He sighed, turned his hand over and gripped mine tight. "All right. I promise I'll do my best to accept it but don't think I won't have my say if he ever does anything to hurt you."

"I'm counting on that. Did you ever do anything to hurt Mama?" He grimaced and I smiled. "No, don't answer that, Papa, I know you did and I know she did things that hurt you, too. No marriage is perfect and there are always some bumps, but if there's love between a husband and wife, that's enough to smooth out the rough spots."

"How'd you get so smart, young lady?"

"Why, from watching you and Mama." I squeezed his hand. "I'm in the mood for biscuits and sausage gravy. How does that sound, Papa?"

"I could eat a couple, I reckon."

"Then I'd better get busy." I slapped my hands down on the table and stood up.

During breakfast, Roy mentioned that he wanted to go up to Sandy Gap Cemetery and check on Mama's and Green's graves. According to Miss Cordy, there'd been a group of hooligans up there with a jug of moonshine and they'd torn down some of the markers.

"Why would they want to do a thing like that?" I asked.

Roy shrugged and nodded to Papa. "Ask Papa, he'd

know better than any of us."

"Since the church was abandoned last year, we've had some trouble up that way. It's far enough away from town that they don't have to worry about getting caught. I don't usually hear about it until after it's done."

"But what about Miss Cordy? She lives up there. Have they been bothering her?"

"Not that I've heard and I talked to her last week when she was in town to do her marketing. Had that pup with her, the one you gave her, Bess, and according to Miss Cordy, he's grown into a fine watch dog. Outgrew his name, that's a fact. Miss Cordy says she's not scared of anything as long as she has Little Bit with her."

I smiled at Fletcher. It may have been me that took Little Bit to Miss Cordy but Fletcher had played a part in saving the dog, too.

"I'll go with you, if you don't mind, Roy," Fletcher said. "You want to come, Bessie?"

"Why don't we all go?" Roy asked.

I should have known something was going on, but I was too busy thinking about stopping to gather wildflowers to place on Mama's, Green's, and Druanna's graves. I knew just the spot, a small clearing in the woods where I'd often stopped in the past to pick flowers for the same reason.

Papa rode his big red mare, Bob, and the rest of us piled into the wagon, Roy driving with Fletcher beside him, Loney, Thee, Jack, and myself in the back. After we stopped to pick the flowers, Fletcher helped Loney up to sit beside Roy and he hopped in the back with me.

That in itself was unusual enough to have me thinking something was going on, but when Fletcher put his arm around me and pulled me close as we drove into the old churchyard, I knew for sure he had another surprise for me.

Sure enough, when we pulled around to the graveyard, I saw it immediately. Papa reined Bob to a stop and sat there, staring at Mama's grave. I blinked, trying without much hope to stem the tears.

I looked up at Fletcher. "You did this?"

"Yeah, I did, with Roy's help, anyway."

"Oh, Fletcher," was all I could get out.

He hopped out of the wagon, held up his arms to help me down. Taking my hand, he walked me over to Mama's grave. The last time I'd seen it, all that had marked it was a handmade wooden cross with her name carved into it but now there was a beautiful marble tombstone that read, Lucinda Henderson Daniels, Beloved Wife, Mother, and Sister, March 12, 1863 – December 20, 1899.

Papa came up beside me, took my other hand. His eyes were wet when he turned to Fletcher and said, "Damn, boy, that's a right fine looking marker. I thank you for it."

"You're welcome, sir."

Papa hesitated then stuck out his right hand. Fletcher shook it as Papa said, "I reckon it's time for you to start calling me by my name." He cleared his throat and gave Fletcher's hand another shake.

"Yes, sir, uh, John."

Papa turned back to me then cocked his head toward the new tombstone sparkling in the sunlight. "Damn, Bess, that's a pretty picture, don't you think? I'd say your mama's pleased as punch up there in heaven." He took off his hat and scratched his head. "Don't know why we didn't think of it ourselves."

I shook my head. "I think maybe it took time for us to get over our grief, and now that we have, we seem to have gotten a little nudge from fate." I winked at my husband. "Or Fate's son, as it were."

Fletch threw back his head and laughed. When Papa clapped him on the shoulder and laughed with him, it sounded to me as if all the angels in heaven were singing.

It brought a smile to my own lips and I glanced up to the sky, hoping Mama was watching and enjoying our merriment.

Fletch and I attended services with my family the next day at Dorland Presbyterian Church, where Pastor Linton preached on the sanctity of family and I felt so blessed to be surrounded by my brothers and sisters, Papa and my husband. I had a fine time chatting with old friends after church and our home that afternoon was filled with people who stopped by to say hello and visit, all bearing food. Miss Cordy brought her sweet dog Little Bit, and Doc Nanny, accompanied by his brother Horace, wearing a bright-purple turban on his head, joined me at the piano with guitar in hand to play for the folks gathered around. Even Tommy Bearing and the Sisters dropped by, and I couldn't help but smile as I noticed the hostile looks Tommy cast my husband. Aunt Belle and Uncle Ned stayed the afternoon, as did Alice, who held Roy's hand, the two whispering together as if no one else in the world existed.

The week passed quickly, as I stayed busy helping Alice and her mother decorate Dorland Chapel for Alice's wedding the following Saturday. Alice's father was short and portly and reminded me of his brother, Hot Springs' Mayor Hill, and her mother seemed an older, more delicate version of the daughter. They had journeyed from Knoxville to see their daughter wed and I thought them highly cultured, impressed at the white roses they ordered from New York for the wedding.

Alice had honored me by asking I stand in as her matron of honor, and when I wasn't with Alice and her mother planning or decorating, I could be found at home entertaining friends who dropped by to visit or with Loney as my sister pinned and pulled at pink, satiny material, shaping it into a dress worthy of our brother's nuptials.

Unlike my own, which had been a simple affair, this wedding was lavishly decorated with hothouse roses, baby's breath and ferns, lilies and pink hydrangeas. White tulle decorated with large pink bows draped between one end of the pews, linking them together, and adorned the large, wooden pulpit. Hundreds of white candles flickered, casting a shifting light onto the dark wood of the chapel, reflecting off pews polished to a glossy sheen and shimmering in the lead-glass windows. Two small flower girls dropped white rosebuds from dainty pink baskets onto a red carpet leading down the aisle between the pews as they led the way for Alice, wearing a long, fitted gown of white silk dotted with pearls and tied with a wide pink sash. Her veil, made of Irish lace, trailed down her back, spilling onto the train of her gown. With her blond hair and blue eyes, I thought her the most beautiful bride I had ever seen, and when I saw Roy's eyes light at the sight of her as she walked toward him, knew he felt the same. Roy looked splendid in his dark-blue suit, white shirt and navy tie, his black hair and eyes glistening in the candlelight, and I thought once more how these two complemented each other, physically as well as mentally. As I had been frightened and anxious as I walked toward my husband, Alice looked to be having a hard time keeping pace with her father. I suspected she wanted to rush headlong into her waiting husband-to-be's arms and was glad these two had found one another.

I suspected most of the town attended the reception at the Mountain Park Hotel. Although the night air was chilly, guests spilled out onto the veranda and were scattered throughout the grounds. A quartet from Knoxville played classical music while guests dined on a never-ending buffet and drank champagne and wine. Afterward, the dances began with Roy and Alice, switching to Roy dancing with Alice's mother and Alice with Papa, looking handsomer than I had ever seen him, and then other dancers quickly joining them on the dance floor. As I spun around with my husband, listening as he whispered in my ear I was the most beautiful woman he'd ever seen, I smiled, thinking how very happy I was and hoping I would always feel this way.

But the next day, after we said our tearful goodbyes and as I boarded the train with Fletch, my mind dwelt on Elisi. I had managed to visit her twice more the past week, accompanied by Fletcher. Although I was glad this gave my great-grandmother the chance to get to know my husband, I was disappointed I couldn't spend time alone with her for more stories and lessons about herbal medicine. It distressed me that each time I saw her, the feeling I would never see her again grew stronger. She had not felt up to attending Roy's wedding, even though I offered for Fletch to fetch her in Papa's wagon, so I hadn't gotten the chance to talk with her one last time, and this weighed heavy on my mind. I reached out for her, telling her how much I loved her and missed her already, and prayed I would have the opportunity to be with her again.

CHAPTER TWELVE

Early Summer 1908

Well, don't that just take the cake?

I stood on the platform at the Old Fort train station, more than seven years married with a now not-so-new house to go along with my not-so-new husband, nervous as a long-tailed cat in a room full of rocking chairs. Shifting anxiously from foot to foot, I waited for the train to arrive, bringing my beloved Papa for a visit.

I could hear the train whistle in the distance and knew it would be a while before it chugged its slow way into the depot, but I looked down the tracks anyway.

"Oh, I wish it would hurry. What in the world's taking it so long?" I said to Fletcher who stood beside me.

He smiled down at me and I had to wonder if he was uneasy about seeing Papa. He didn't appear to be but with Fletcher it was sometimes hard to tell what was going on in his head.

At another blast of the whistle, still far away from the station, I turned and leaned out over the tracks again, peering into the distance, willing it to appear around the nearest bend.

Fletcher clasped my elbow. "Careful there, Bess, or you'll fall."

My nerves were frazzled, my mind careening between anticipation and worry about how Papa would act when he saw our little house. I'd worked so hard to get it ready for him and wanted him to see that Fletcher and I were building a good life together but was concerned that he'd take one look and walk away in disgust—as he had when Fletcher had tried to ask for his blessing of our marriage.

This time, I vowed, I wouldn't go after him if he did. I was a married woman now and I didn't need his approval.

But that didn't stop me from wanting it.

Fletcher's hand moved to the small of my back and I jumped. He chuckled. "I think you had too much of that coffee this morning, Bessie. What in the Sam hill are you so fidgety about?"

I merely shook my head and looked down the track again. I didn't answer because I didn't want to hurt his feelings, which I was sure I would do if he knew how much I wanted my father's good opinion.

I'd even prayed for it the night before, lying in bed, wide awake, asking God to make Papa see my life the way I saw it, as a building up, a journey in progress which would only get better as time went by.

I sighed and Fletcher rubbed his hand over my back. "Are you excited or nervous, Bess?"

"A little of both," I admitted as I leaned my head on his shoulder and listened to the train whistle again. "It sure didn't seem to take us this long to get here when we were on it."

He laughed. "No, I don't suppose it did."

"It seems as if it's taking forever this time," I said.

"Sure does but it'll get here soon." He took his hand off my back and tipped his hat. "Afternoon, Mr. Denby."

"You going or waiting?" Mr. Denby asked Fletcher as he tipped his hat to me. "Missus Bessie."

I smiled at him as Fletcher said, "We're waiting for Bessie's father. He's coming in from Hot Springs today. How about you?"

Mr. Denby hitched up his pants. "Wife's coming in from Asheville. She's been visiting our daughter, helping out with the new baby." He nodded in the direction of the tracks. "Here she comes."

I turned and, sure enough, you could finally see the large locomotive, steam pouring from its stack and trailing alongside the other cars like a frothy white ribbon. My stomach did a slow roll at the same time my heart seemed to leap into my throat. Papa! Papa was here. I clutched Fletcher's hand as the train pulled into the station, praying my father would at last accept my marriage.

It wasn't long after we got home that I realized my prayers weren't to be answered, or perhaps, I should say, I wasn't to get the answer I'd hoped for.

Papa stood in my kitchen warming his hands by the stove which I had proudly showed off to him, hoping he'd see it as a sign that my life was going in the right direction. "Bess, you know damn good and well you weren't never used to anything like this. You could do a hell of a lot better." It disappointed me he only saw that our house wasn't anywhere near as nice as the ones he'd built while I was growing up.

But I wouldn't let myself get mad and say something disrespectful, I only smiled, leaned over and kissed his cheek. I blinked back tears when his handlebar moustache tickled. That feather light brushing brought back so many memories for me, the many times I'd kissed him in that exact same spot as I was growing up, the many times he'd gathered me in his arms to comfort me or reassure me of his love.

I stepped back and took his hand, squeezing until he looked at me. "I'm happy, Papa, and I hope you'll be happy for me. We may not have much yet but we're getting along fairly well. Besides, we're young, and if we work hard, we can have anything we want." I turned and pointed out the open back door. "That land out there, as far as the eye can see and even farther, is all ours. 400 acres bought and paid for." I swept my arm. "We have friends and family on the mountain and down in Old Fort who keep us company or help when needed. And we have a church just a little ways up the main road where we can worship God and ask for his blessings if we need them." I turned back and looked at him. "What more do we need, Papa?"

He shook his head. "I wanted more for you, Bess, that's all, more than working your fingers to the bone and scrabbling for the niceties of life."

I shook my head. I had everything I needed and a husband I loved to share it with, but this was Papa and he could be blind when it came to his children. I reached out and put my hand on his cheek. "I know you did, Papa, and I appreciate that but I have what I want. Can't my happiness be enough for you?"

"I reckon it'll have to be. You're married to him now and there ain't nothing to be done about it." He looked around the kitchen again and scowled.

"Oh, Papa," I sighed, "you and Mama didn't have everything you wanted when you first married, did you?"

"We sure had a damn sight more than this. And I had a job with a paycheck."

"Maybe so, but it took you plenty of years before you owned your own house and even more years before you had enough money to consider yourself well-off. Money isn't everything, Papa. I'll take happiness over money any day of the week. I don't need fancy clothes or a fancy house or a lot of money to be happy."

He turned away, looked out the window. "You look healthy anyway."

"I am and so is Fletcher. And I love everything about teaching. I have good days when the children are little angels and I can't think of anything else I'd want to be doing. I have bad days, too, when they're more like little demons, but even on those days they give me a reason to smile. And the feeling that runs over me when I see that light in their eyes that means they finally figured out what I'm teaching them, well, I can't describe it." I laughed. "Well, look at me, gushing like the geyser but really, it's nothing short of amazing and never fails to thrill me."

"That's good. You always were good with the young'uns."

I nodded. "True, I was and I still am, even if some of them are bigger than I am. But I love teaching at Cedar Grove and being able to come home every night. It sure is better than having to stay through the week with the family of one of my students like I did when I first started teaching."

He frowned at that and I regretted bringing up the fact that the first five years of my teaching career had been in a school too far away for the daily walk. He just couldn't understand how I could be happy living with the family of one of my students during the week and with my husband's family the rest of the time. He and Mama had never been separated for more than a night the entire time they'd been married.

I was determined not to let Papa's disapproval get to me so changed the subject. "Would you like to see the rest of the place, Papa?"

"I reckon I would." He walked over to the door and looked out the small window. "Who lives in that sha—house next door?"

"No one. Fletcher's going to tear it down when he gets the chance. When we first bought the property, we were thinking about connecting it to this house to make it bigger, but after Fletcher got a good look at it, he said it was best to tear it down and we could build on to this house if we needed more room."

He nodded and pulled the door open. "Well, let's go see what's what."

I followed him out the door and for once left the hoe leaning against the door jamb. If I carried it with me, Papa would probably want to know why, and when I explained it was for protection against snakes, he would frown and most likely offer to give me his gun. That or read Fletcher the riot act that night about him not taking good care of me. Since I'd married Fletch, I had to keep up a constant balancing act between him and Papa. I hated to admit it, but sometimes I was glad for the distance that separated us.

Taking Papa's arm, I led him toward the big cantilevered barn out back. "This is Fletcher's pride and joy. Oh, you should have heard the teasing he got from the men at the barn raising when he showed them his plans." I laughed at the memory then sobered when I remembered little Gerald Davis being bitten by the rattlesnake.

"What do you do to keep busy, Bess?"

"Oh, I help Fletcher where I can, milk the cows and feed

the chickens, gather the eggs, and believe it or not, I've been sewing. I'm not really good yet, but I'm improving."

He looked at me in surprise. "Damn, Bess, I never thought to see you with a needle and thread in your hands."

I laughed. "Needs must, Papa."

"I reckon but you sewing just don't seem right somehow. Maybe I had one of your Mama's feelings when I loaded up that old sewing machine and toted it all the way over the mountains on the train."

Papa had arrived on the train bearing gifts; the sewing machine he had received in lieu of taxes from Mr. Sullivan and a big white box which he'd placed on his bed, refusing to tell me what was in it when I asked.

"Maybe you did, Papa, but I think it probably has more to do with me writing to Loney and asking her the proper way to darn a sock. When Fletcher and I first arrived here, the mountain women were sort of stand-offish and considered me a big-city girl." I laughed and shook my head. "After seeing how they shied away from me, I vowed not to let any of them know how scared and inexperienced I was. My first step was to learn to sew so I wouldn't have to hire it out and give them another reason to think I was some spoiled city girl. I took up a needle and one of Fletcher's shirts that he'd managed to rip and went from there. The one thing I couldn't figure out how to do was darn a darn sock so I wrote and asked Loney." I laughed again. "Believe me, it was a complete surprise to find that I enjoy sewing. Most of the time, anyway. It's relaxing and, like canning, satisfying. Most likely, that's because I haven't tackled anything too hard, just some mending mostly, but I did buy a pattern at the general store last year when Fletcher came home with some material and I made a dress for me and a shirt for him. Both were simple enough but, I swan, my fingers were sore from all the needle pricks. I'm getting better though and the sewing machine will help once I learn how to use it."

"You haven't taken up quilting, have you?"

"Oh no, nothing that complicated, but who knows, maybe one day I will. And thanks to Aunt Belle's generosity when we got married, we have enough quilts to last us for a good long while."

We went into the cool barn and I was happy to note Papa seemed to approve Fletch's improvements when he inspected them.

He ran his hand over the half door of one of the stalls. "Fletcher going to get himself another horse?"

"Oh, I don't know. We have the mare and the two mules, but maybe when the tobacco crop comes in and he sells it, he might decide we need another one."

"You say he's growing tobacco?"

"Yes, that was the first thing he did after we bought the property. He cleared some land and planted half an acre. It isn't a lot but it does bring in some money every fall."

"Good, then he should buy a horse for you and maybe you won't have to walk back and forth to school every day. Gotta be hard in the winter when it's cold. I'd say it snows a lot more here than it does in Hot Springs since you're higher up than us."

"I don't mind the walk, Papa. It isn't far at all, and some days, usually when it's raining, I ride Fletcher's mare. Now, when I was working at Crooked Creek, that was a walk, but I didn't mind that so much, either. I was raring to go on Sunday afternoon just to get away from all the noise at the Elliotts' house and have some peace and quiet. I could always find that in the woods."

He frowned again then shook his head and chuckled. "You always were one for your quiet time. Reckon that won't ever change."

I laughed with him. "No, Papa, I don't think it ever will. That's how I'm made, I guess. Why, Fletcher even set aside one corner of the barn loft for me so I would have a place of my own just like I did at home."

"He did, huh? Well, that's something he done right."

"Oh, Papa, don't be so hard on him. He's doing his best and I'd say he's doing a fine job making me happy. I really hoped when he got Mama's tombstone and put it on her grave you had put all that behind you."

He grunted but didn't say anything else. We continued to stroll around the barn and I showed him my thriving grape vines, the flourishing garden, and the outhouse Fletcher had repaired as we talked about family and friends in Hot Springs. When we got back to the kitchen, I told Papa to sit and went about starting a pot of coffee.

After I got it on the stove, I turned and said, "What's bothering you, Papa?"

He sighed. "You're your mother's daughter all right. I've got something to tell you, Bess."

I waited but he didn't say anything for the longest time. Finally I said, "What is it, Papa?"

Clearing his throat, he stroked his moustache and then said, "Well, ah, I'm moving the family to Knoxville, Bess."

"Knoxville," was all I could get past the lump in my throat.

"It's farther away from you but the train runs clear from there to here so I'll still be able to come see you when you want and you'll be able to come see us, too." He looked down at the dog sunning himself in a beam of sunshine beside the table. "I don't want to but I, damn, Bess, I need to."

I didn't think he'd tell me but asked anyway, "Why, Papa?"

Taking off his hat, he wiped his forearm across his forehead then scrubbed his hand over his face. I took pity on him but still wanted to hear him say it. Catching his hand, stopping the up and down motion, I said, "Why, Papa, why do you need to move to Knoxville?"

He sighed and looked me straight in the eye. "I need to get out of Hot Springs. I finished the house and there are a few people interested in buying it. I haven't found any property suitable for building and can't find a house that needs to be fixed up so..." he shrugged, "I figured this was the time to go."

"Is that the only reason, Papa?"

"Damn, Bess, you always were too smart for your own good. I need to get away from the memories of your mama. I did fine for a while, well, after I got the first part of my grieving done, but now that Roy's married and working with the railroad and Loney's all grown up and looking to marry..."

I knew about Roy's job, of course, but this was the first I'd heard about Loney getting married. "Loney's getting married? She hasn't said anything about it in her letters to me."

"No, no, not yet, she doesn't even have a beau but she's looking and she has that job at the Mountain Park." He snorted out his disgust. "Cleaning rooms. Says she only wants to earn a little money of her own but I know she's got her eye on those fancy tourists from up north."

Looking down to hide my smile, I said, "Papa, Loney's a grown woman now. You have to let her make her own way in the world."

"I know, Bessie. I may be a cantankerous old cuss but I let you do what you wanted, didn't I?"

"Well, you came around to it eventually." I smiled to show him I didn't really hold any of that against him. And if he needed to get away from all the memories of Mama in Hot Springs, I certainly could understand that. I'd had the same trouble more than a few times after she and Green had died. Leaving Hot Springs hadn't taken the memories away for me but it had softened them a bit. "Moving to Knoxville won't take the memories away, Papa."

"I know that, girl, but I, oh, hell, Bessie, I need to do this."

"All right, if you feel it's for the best, I think you should."

He brightened a little at that. "I will, and don't you worry about your Papa or the rest of the family. I see notices in the paper all the time about them needing men to work on rebuilding the downtown area after it burned to the ground back in '97. I shouldn't have any trouble getting work and I'll take the money from selling the house and put it in another house in Knoxville, maybe even have enough for two. That should keep me busy enough."

I nodded. "I'm sure it will. I'll miss you, Papa."

"Hell, girl, I'm not going to some foreign country. I'm only going one state over, we'll practically be neighbors."

"I know, Papa, but I'll still miss you and the rest of the family."

"Well, I'll miss you, too, but like I said, you can come to visit after we get settled. We'll come visit you, too, when we can. Only takes a few hours on the train."

"All right," I agreed even though it hurt my heart to think about no one being close enough to visit with Mama and Green. Who would look after their graves, take them flowers in the spring, spend time talking to them and telling them what was happening with the family? I had done that when I lived in Hot Springs and I knew Loney and Aunt Belle often did those things after I left, but with Loney in Knoxville and Aunt Belle getting older, I wondered who would tend their graves. I sent a small prayer up to God to keep Aunt Belle healthy so she would be able to visit her beloved sister and see to her grave.

After a supper of chicken and dumplings, which Papa praised as pert-near as good as Mama's, we went in the small living room to have coffee. Papa disappeared for a moment, going to the spare bedroom where he would sleep.

I stood by the sewing machine, pondering what had made Papa bring it to me. I wasn't known for my sewing skills, as a matter of fact, I was known for my lack of them, but Papa for some reason had decided I needed the machine more than Loney. Of course, Loney could sew a dress in short time by hand so maybe that was what he'd been thinking.

As if reading my thoughts, Papa said, "Loney's got her eyes set on one of those new-fangled electric sewing machines. I figured I'd see about getting her one once we're living in Knoxville." His gaze darted around our small home, which would not see electricity for many years, and I felt his disappointment once more over my lifestyle.

Ignoring that, I ran my hands over the top, thinking about when Papa had taken the sewing machine in lieu of taxes from Mr. Sullivan. I'd gone with him that bright fall morning as I often did when he made his rounds to collect taxes and we'd had a wonderful day, talking of the townspeople, the approaching winter, and other things that crossed our minds. It was shortly after I met Fletcher for the first time at my Uncle Robert's farm in Walnut and was questioning my reaction to him and whether or not I could ever love another man as much as Papa. I had tried to talk to him about that but hadn't been able to bring myself to tell him what was on my mind. Papa, however, sensed that I was worried about something and eventually drew it out of me.

I looked up as he walked back in the room, carrying the large white box in his hands.

"What in the world is in that box, Papa?"

He pointed to the sewing machine. "You learned to use that yet, girl?"

I waved my hand in the air. "Oh, I'm halfway through my first quilt."

He winked. "That's my girl. You always were a bright one, Bessie, you'll learn in no time." He held the box out to me. "This is for you, Bessie. It, uh..." he coughed. "It's from your mama. She set it aside to give to you when you married. I, well, I'm sorry I didn't think about it before." He cut his eyes at Fletcher then back to me as he shook his head. "No excuse, except an old man's contrary nature. Sit down over there, Bess."

When I did, he placed the box on my lap. "Go ahead, open it."

I stared at it, running my hands over the top. "It's from Mama? What in the world?"

Papa cleared his throat then grinned. "Open it and see." He laughed when I only shook my head and stared at him. "It ain't gonna bite you, girl."

I opened the box and found a beautiful white quilt covered with embroidered images that looked like scenes of people and places linked together with a twining of leaves running from one to the next, connecting them like a path through the woods. A shiver chased up my spine and I looked at Papa questioningly.

"Here," Papa said and pulled it from the box. "Get up from there, boy, I need your chair for a minute," he said to Fletcher. When Fletcher stood up, Papa shook out the quilt and spread it over the chair so we could get a better look at it.

I walked over and gasped as the chill intensified till I actually shook with it. Fletcher came over to stand beside me, studying the quilt, too.

Mama had done this for me, starting with an announcement of the birth of Vashti Lee Daniels on January 17, 1881, the leaf-studded vine leading from that to the next picture and on to the next. I leaned over, ran my hand over the stitching, following the vine, stopping at an embroidered building that looked eerily like the Dorland Institute Chapel where Fletch and I had been married.

My fingers trembled as I flattened my hand over the stained glass window of the church and I knew this was a map of my life.

Papa put a hand on my shoulder. "Cindy called it a Magic Quilt, Bess. It's all the things she wanted to happen for you in your life and, well, according to your great-grandmother and your Aunt Belle, it's magic because it tells what's going to happen before it even happens." He cleared his throat again. "Hell, I reckon I may as well come right out and say it, it ain't no secret the women in your mama's family have a gift for seeing into the future. Cindy started work on this while she was carrying you, before you were born. She made one for all of her girls, you, Loney, and she started one for Jack, but she didn't have time to finish that one so your Aunt Belle did."

"But how? I mean, how could she know what would happen in my life?" I shook my head. "How could she know I'd be a girl before I was even born?"

He shrugged. "She said once she knew you were coming she started having dreams about you, about things that would happen in your life. Same thing with Loney and Jack. She wouldn't tell me what she dreamed, said she didn't want to set the gremlins to your life." He chuckled. "Far as I know, it never happened with her boys for some reason, but she got those feelings with every one of her girls."

He pointed to the first embroidered scene on the quilt, the one that started the journey. "She had that done before you were born. And see this here?" His hand moved to the next scene. "That's the house we were living in when you were born." He traced his fingers to the next. "And see here, that's our first home in Hot Springs. You remember that, don't you?"

"Yes, we lived in the back and upstairs, and Mr. Lance used the front as a store."

"That's right and here," he traced to the next, a heart with one word embroidered in it, *Bessie.* "That's when you changed your name."

"But Mama never called me that, she always called me Vashti. I thought she hated the name Bessie."

"Nope, not hated it though she may have preferred Vashti since that was the name she gave you, but looking at this, you can see she knew you were going to be Bessie and maybe she knew that was the right name for you."

"But why didn't she just go ahead and name me Bessie?"

"Hell, Bess, how do I know? Your mama was a puzzle to me most of the time and when you threw in those Cherokee traits she inherited I was completely stumped, but all she would tell me was not to question the old ways. I had no idea what she meant by that and she couldn't explain it so I just let it go."

The old ways, I knew that meant the Cherokee ways. If I had learned anything from Elisi, it was that the Cherokee ways were all about finding the path you were meant to walk in life.

I traced the heart with my finger and sent up a silent apology to Mama. It wasn't the first plea for forgiveness I'd sent winging into the heavens nor would it be the last. I had misjudged her so horribly when she was alive but thought I understood her right before and after she died. Apparently, I was wrong, and judging by this quilt, I hadn't even scratched the surface of the woman who was my mother, a woman whom I hadn't learned to appreciate until it was far too late.

Continuing to trace the vine, my fingers drifted over a diploma with my name on it, a red ear of corn, followed by the bridge on Bridge Street spanning Spring Creek where Fletcher had proposed to me, coming to a stop over the chapel where we married. "This wasn't built until the year after she died," I murmured. Oh, how I wished she'd lived to see it, she would have loved the colorful stained glass windows and the way the chapel sparkled with vibrant rainbows on a sunny day. Next on the quilt there was a train which had to signify that train ride to Old Fort after Fletcher and I married, and after that a school bell just like the one Fletcher gave me

My fingers stilled over the next image, a small house with a creek running in front and a cantilevered barn in the back with a row of grapevines along the fence leading to the house, and beside it, a crooked row of shacks. Fletcher put an arm around my shoulders, and when I looked up at him, he nodded.

"That looks like our land all right, Bessie."

I went back to the quilt, searching the rest of the images Mama had so lovingly stitched, a shelf with tins of dried herbs and a one-room school house. I knew what those meant but the ones that followed were a mystery. An organ, another larger schoolhouse, a young boy, an empty tombstone, a full moon riding high in a dark blue sky, and a large building which looked to be built of brick, all connected with the twining vine. My heart turned over when I realized, with the exception of the young boy, there didn't seem to be any indication of children in my future. Did that mean Fletcher and I would not be blessed with any? If I was to have a baby, wouldn't Mama have stitched something indicating it, like a little bootie or a nursing bottle or something like that? I felt sure she would have but instead she had stitched a young school-age boy. What did that mean?

Drawing in a shaky breath, I turned my face into Fletcher's chest, rested there for a moment.

"You all right, Bess?" Fletcher asked.

I nodded then looked up at him, tried to gauge if he'd noticed the lack of children in our future. He pulled me fully into his arms and whispered in my ear, "It's all right, she made this before you were even born and maybe she missed some things."

"Maybe," I murmured. "Maybe she did." I drew back and looked into his eyes. "I certainly hope so."

And I knew right then my days of chewing the seeds of Queen Anne's Lace were over. I would no longer actively avoid getting pregnant. Instead, I vowed to do everything I could to see that I would conceive at least one child and hopefully more than that. Children were, after all, the only true way Fletcher and I had of leaving a legacy behind in this world.

Papa, apparently picking up on my despair, placed his hand on my back above Fletcher's arms and rubbed. "She missed you dancing in the saloon in Paint Rock, didn't she, girl? And that fight Norton had with the Yankee. Remember that, the one where you were ready to take that northerner on to get justice for Norton?" He laughed but sobered quickly at the next thought. "She missed the flash flood and..." he cleared his throat, "our little Green. And she missed Druanna," he added quietly.

Yes, she had missed Green's awful death—had it been because she hadn't known at the time that she would have Green, I wondered—and she had missed Druanna, too, the Melungeon girl whose death had driven a wedge between Papa and me that had lasted until I married. If she'd missed those two events, two that I considered to be maybe not the most significant but certainly among the most important happenings in my life, she could have missed a couple of children.

She'd also missed the birth of little Jack, and her own death following quickly after that. And again, I had to wonder if it was because those things were hidden to her somehow or maybe it was because they were her life and not mine. I never had visions or feelings about my own life so maybe Mama hadn't either.

I sighed. It was one more thing I wished I could talk to Elisi about. If only she didn't live so far away.

Tears came to my eyes at the thought and I picked up the quilt, folded it and ran my fingers over the bumps made by the colorful thread, stopping at the picture of the young boy. I didn't know what he signified but somehow knew he'd play an important role in my life...whoever he was.

CHAPTER THIRTEEN

Summer 1908

Even a blind hog finds an acorn now and then.

Summer in the mountains brought hot, humid days where it felt as if I were drawing hot water into my lungs and my body would be coated with beads of moisture as soon as I stepped outside but sometimes Mother Nature would grace us with mornings cool and refreshing leading to breezy afternoons that would lift the hair and cool the skin. The morning began nice enough and I hoped would be a prelude to one of those perfect days, so after I finished my chores, I decided it would be a good time for picking grapes. School would start up again in a few weeks and when it did I would spend the majority of my time inside teaching, surrounded by my students, so days comfortable enough to be outside were meant to be spent there. Fletcher had left early that morning to cut lumber to sell and probably wouldn't return until late afternoon, and I felt a bit giddy at having a day to myself. Mayhap I could even spend time in my barn loft reading or writing in my journal.

The fence Fletch built along the path leading from our small cabin to the barn proved to be the perfect place for my grapevines. They grew quickly, weaving their way over and between the wooden rails, and flourished there from the day I planted them until I left my old home place, producing gallons of the sweet, juicy fruit. Over the years, I've often wondered what happened to those grapevines and hope they're still there to this day, giving their owner the gift of a delicious treat during the summer.

Basket in one hand and my trusty hoe in the other, I made my way down the path, the sun feeling warm against my back as I breathed in the sweet mountain air, humming *Swing Low, Sweet Chariot* because I'd heard the ghosts again the night before.

I didn't see the man until I was almost on top of him and when I noticed him startled, stepping back and dropping the basket as I tightened my grip on the hoe.

A frightened look crossed his face and he stepped back as well, wringing the hat he held in his hand in agitation. "I – I'm so sorry, ma'am, I shore didn't mean to scare you."

I glanced around, wondering if I should be afraid of him, but he seemed meek enough. I had become comfortable enough with my gift by then to take note when it spoke to me and sensed nothing dangerous about this situation. When I saw a woman and two small children close by, I relaxed. "Who are you?" I asked, studying the man, broad in stature with skin black as coal.

He darted a look at his family before turning back to me. "My name's George, ma'am, and I don't suppose I could bother you for some food? My family and me, we've been on the road a good while and my girls..." He looked back at his family.

I studied the two girls, clinging to their mama's skirts, and my heart broke at their dirty clothes, skinny arms and legs grimy with dust from their travels. I smiled to put them at ease, saying, "Come inside and I'll fix you and your family something to eat."

Relief flooded his eyes as he nodded. "If'n you don't mind, ma'am, why, we'll just wait out there. Don't want to be bothering you none."

"Oh, pshaw, it's too hot out here to stand in the sun for long. Come on inside where it's cooler."

Stuffing the hat back on his head, he bent down to retrieve my basket. "I'll pick all this up for you, ma'am. I'm so sorry, I shore didn't mean to scare you."

I waved at his wife, calling "Come on in the house, let's get some food into those young'uns of yours." His wife hesitated at first but the two girls tugging at her hands finally got her moving.

I stepped onto the back porch and into the kitchen then went directly to the stove and began stoking the fire. I smiled at his wife as she paused in the doorway. "Come on in and get out of that hot sun. You can sit there at the table and rest while I put together some food for you."

"I thank you, ma'am," she said, her eyes on the floor.

I smiled at George as he came through the doorway and stepped over to his wife, holding out my hand. "My name's Bessie. Bessie Elliott."

She stared at my hand like it was a snake. Her husband moved in front of her and gave me one quick shake. "This is my wife Sadie."

"Nice to meet you, Sadie." I smiled at the two girls. Both were such pretty little things with wide, dark eyes and black, curly hair. One looked to be about eight, the other five or six. "And what are your names?"

The youngest ducked behind her mama but the oldest darted a glance at me, giving me a quick smile. "My name's Liza and my sister's Ruth."

"Very nice to meet you, Liza and Ruth." I returned to the stove and began cracking eggs into my iron skillet.

"Um, ma'am?"

I turned around and nodded at George.

"You sure your man's gonna be all right with you havin' us here, inside your home?"

"Why wouldn't he be? I don't see that you're any danger. And we don't turn anyone away who's hungry and in need."

"Thank you, ma'am, we shore do appreciate it."

"Have a seat, George." I waited while he settled into a chair, looking uncomfortable. I smiled at Liza. "How about eggs, biscuits and ham? You feel up to eating some of that?"

Her eyes lit with pleasure. "Oh, yes, ma'am. We're near starved to death. We ain't had no food in—"

"We is hungry, ma'am," George interrupted, giving her a warning look.

I turned my back to them while I cooked, saying over my shoulder. "Where are y'all from?"

"Down South Carolina way," George answered.

I smiled to myself. "My papa's from South Carolina. And his papa was a hog drover who drove hogs from Greeneville, Tennessee to Greenville, South Carolina. Are you going anywhere specific, George?"

It took awhile for George to answer. He finally said, "No, ma'am, just looking for a place to settle, somewhere I can get me some work and support my family."

"How long have y'all been on the road?"

"Oh, I reckon about a month now."

I couldn't imagine what it would be like, traveling by foot with a wife and two small children. Apparently they had no money. How had they been feeding themselves? From the looks of them, not very well at all. "And you haven't found anything before now?"

"No, ma'am, ain't havin' much luck."

Fletcher had mentioned that morning he sure wouldn't mind having another man around the place, someone to help him with the farming and lumbering. He wanted to get into the cattle and hog business, and I knew with the plans he had for our farm, he wouldn't be able to do it by himself. George might be a good worker for him. He looked hardy enough.

I scraped the scrambled eggs into a bowl, placed the leftover ham and biscuits from breakfast onto a platter, and set the food down in front of them, adding the grapes I'd picked that morning. "I've got milk if you want some," I said, watching the two little girls struggle not to grab food and stuff it into their mouths.

"That'd be mighty nice," George said.

"Go ahead, eat," I encouraged as I poured milk into tin mugs for them then busied myself tidying up the stove, listening to them devour the food behind me.

When I heard chairs scraping back, I turned around. "You full up? If not, I can fix something else for you."

George smiled at me, his teeth bright and white in that dark face. "Oh, no, ma'am, I reckon we got our fill." He patted his stomach for emphasis. "But I do thank you. That shore was good." He rose to his feet, signaling to his wife to do likewise. "Well, I reckon we best be gettin' on outside. I want to thank you, again, Mrs. Elliott, for that fine meal." He hesitated at the door and turned back. "I'd be more than happy to repay you by doin' any chores you need done around here." I didn't miss the hopeful plea in his eyes.

I smiled, happy at this. This would hopefully delay them until Fletcher got home and I could talk to him about hiring George.

"Well, my husband's gone, cutting timber on the mountain, but I sure could use more kindling chopped if you've a mind to."

"Why, I reckon I wouldn't mind one bit, Mrs. Fletcher."

"Please, call me Bessie." I looked at his wife. "And you, too, Sadie. No need for formalities here."

For the first time her lips lifted in a smile.

George stuffed his ragged hat back on his head. "Well, I guess I better be gettin' to it, then." He started for the door, his wife and their two girls following close behind.

"Sadie," I called. She turned and gave me a questioning look. "If you and your girls want to rest, you can use one of our shacks across the way. They're all empty but they're clean. I figured you might want to nap or perhaps you and your girls might want to bathe or put on some fresh clothes."

Sadie's eyes clouded. "We thank you for your kindness, Miss Bessie, but the only clothes we gots is the ones on our backs." She gave a curt nod at my look of surprise. "We got robbed a few weeks back."

Oh, that wouldn't do. "Well, you go on over to one of those cabins and rest while I see what I can scrounge up for you and your girls."

George shook his head. "Oh, no, Miss Bessie, you done enough for us. We can't take no more of your charity."

"Why, I reckon you'd do the same for me, George, if I were in similar circumstances. Now, go on. Sadie, if you want to bathe, there's a big washtub in the first cabin and you can fetch water from the creek."

She reached out her hand as if to touch me then quickly drew it back. "Miss Bessie, you're too kind. I thank you from my heart."

"Go on, now, we've all got things to do." I turned my back so she wouldn't see my moist eyes. What a horrible life they must have, to be on the road with nothing of value, no family apparently to help them out. Well, they'll have family now, I thought with determination. There was room enough for them here and Lord knows enough work to go around for everyone. If they stayed, that is.

Shortly enough I heard an axe biting into wood and smiled to myself. In our chiffarobe, I found an old dress I hadn't worn in a good while. It would be too long for Sadie but I could shorten it. Although it was frayed in places, it held up good and should do her until we could find more clothes. Maybe the other women from church could donate material or dresses, I thought, as I rummaged for something for the children. I finally decided two old shirts of Fletcher's would do. They could wear these while I washed and dried their clothes. They'd probably drag the ground but they were all we had.

I carried the clothes across to the cabin, smiling at George as I passed by.

He wiped sweat off his brow and nodded at me. "God bless you, Miss Bessie."

"Thank you, George, and God bless you." I knocked on the doorjamb of the cabin then stepped inside, where I found Liza and Ruth shivering in the washtub while Sadie scrubbed their skin. Even though it was summer, the water from the creek was still biting cold. "You got yourself two pretty little girls," I said, wondering if I'd ever be blessed with children. The girls giggled and squirmed, anxious to be out of the water and playing, I was sure. I placed the clothes on the old wooden table in the center of the cabin. "Sadie, I found a dress that should do you but don't have anything for the girls but some old shirts of my husband's. I figured they could wear these until we get their clothes washed and dried."

"Oh," Sadie said, brushing her hand along the dress I brought. "Why, this is the prettiest thing I've ever seen," she said, holding the yellow dress against her body. "I ain't never had a dress so pretty."

"Yellow's a good color for you," I replied, thanking God for Fletcher and all we had and that I had never faced times such as these people. I gathered the girls' clothes. "I'll wash these while y'all bathe and change. As warm as it is outside today, I reckon they'll be dry soon enough. Sadie, I'll wash yours when you're ready."

"Thank you, ma'am," she said softly behind me as I bustled outside. I stopped for a moment and turned my face to the sky. It felt good to be helping these people, I thought, and wondered what Fletcher would say when he came home and found a Negro family staying in one of our shacks. A twinge of guilt swept through me when I realized the shack they were in had originally been part of the slave quarters. The cabins were in disrepair when we moved onto the plantation but Fletcher had fixed them up so they were livable, hoping that some day we would have workers or sharecroppers living in them. This just might be our first family to share our farm with us and I was happy at the thought.

By the time Fletcher returned, George had produced a good-sized pile of kindling for my wood stove and was stacking it against the cabin when Fletcher walked by. I stood by the kitchen window watching as Fletcher gave George a curious look as he nodded at him, not seeming startled at the sight of a colored man making a woodpile.

George said, "Evening, sir," and went right on with his chore.

Fletcher stepped into the kitchen, taking off his hat and wiping sweat off his forehead. He didn't say anything, simply arched his brows in an inquisitive way. "That's George," I said, pointing outside. "He and his wife and two little girls have been on the road for a month looking for work. They were near starved to death so I fed them some lunch and he asked to do some chores to pay me back."

"Mark of a good man and I'm glad he did," Fletcher said, washing his hands and splashing water on his face. "Saved me a lot of trouble."

"They've been robbed, Fletch. Only have the clothes on their backs. No money, no food." I shook my head. "This world can be a real cruel place sometimes."

Fletcher watched me for a moment and his eyes lit as if he knew exactly what I was thinking. "I been needing another man around here to help out. You reckon he'd stay if I asked?"

"Don't see why not," I said with a grin. "You're not as ornery as you look."

He nodded. "It'd be the Christian thing to do, I reckon." He put his hat back on his head. "I'll go talk to him."

I watched as the two men conferred, their voices drowned out by squeals as Liza and Ruth chased each other on the other side of the creek. Sadie sat on the front steps of the small cabin, smiling at her little girls' cheerfulness. Fletcher spoke for awhile, waving his arms around our place, pointing out the mountains around us, the acreage that had been cleared for a large garden, the seeds we had planted just now showing results. I marveled at how much Fletch had done himself and wondered why in the world we hadn't hired someone to help before now. When the two men shook hands, George with a big smile on his face, I knew the deed was done and we had hired our first helper.

Little did I know what a godsend George would prove to be to us nor what a curse we would be to him.

CHAPTER FOURTEEN

Late Summer 1908

She ain't worth the salt in her bread.

After Cedar Grove Church closed, Fletcher and I decided to join Stone Mountain Baptist Church, where his family attended, but more importantly because it was the only church on Stone Mountain. Although I had been raised Presbyterian, a religion I found not so confining as the Baptists, I came to like it well enough after I was asked to play the piano during services, which I enjoyed more than listening to the preacher's pontifications about hellfire and damnation. Fletch was proud when the congregation asked him to perform the services of a deacon so we became active parishioners and were present during most worship services.

Reverend Charles Ecclesiastes Redmon had been pastor there for over two and a half years and seemed to enjoy his flock of worshippers although found them a bit pale in comparison to past congregations. Fletcher quickly became his favored deacon and the reverend told me I made the best Sunday chicken dinner he'd ever tasted. This always put me in mind of poor Miss Cordy and her pet hen, and as I fried chicken for the reverend, I'd say a silent prayer for that sweet woman and her dog Little Bit back in Hot Springs.

Reverend Redmon spoke often about how his past congregations had always been a lively bunch, stomping their feet, waving their hands and shouting out, with an occasional parishioner talking in tongues, but this flock was nothing but sedate and seemed more prone to nodding off during his sermons than offering up thunderous cries of *Amen* or *Hallelujah* and *Praise the Lord.* He wanted to shake up the worshippers, maybe scare them a little so they'd be more expressive, and constantly contemplated how he could do this. Finally, he confided in Fletch, who was known for his handiwork, that he had come up with an idea and asked him to help build a lever system under the church so that when the reverend stepped on a small, wooden pad behind the altar, a thumping sound would be heard in the aisle in front of the altar.

The good reverend chose a revival night to execute his plan. The church was perhaps half-full and the night cloudy and warm. The church door was propped open to capture any cool air that came down the hollow and kerosene lanterns were lit and placed on small shelves lining the side walls. As usual, I sat at the piano in front of the church. My seat put me in direct sight of the reverend and his small wooden pad and I was curious what sort of reaction he'd get. After he welcomed everyone and lead in the singing of *The Old Rugged Cross*, he looked sternly around at every person and said, "I tell you truthfully that ole Satan is loose in this world and he gits in our heads and makes us do all kinds of evil and crazy stuff. He's been here on Broad River and he had a hand in the stealin' of the clothes off'n the wider Elzey's clothesline, includin' some fancy underwear, I'm told." Elzey hid her red face in her hands as tittering, oftentimes covered by coughs, spread throughout the congregation. Reverend Redmon raised his hand. "I'm tellin' you that..." I watched as he stepped down on the pad behind the altar and a loud thump, thump, thump rebounded around the room. At the same time, a gust of wind blew the church door closed and caused the lamps to flicker. Startled gasps and anxious murmurings could be heard as everyone stared at the floor in front of the altar.

A smile flickered across Reverend Redmon's face and I watched as he darted an appreciative look toward Fletcher, standing in the back of the room, before opening his eyes wide and looking over the altar at the floor. "What was that?" he boomed. He walked down to the aisle in front of the altar and threw himself onto the floor and put his ear against the planks. Everyone stared at him with rapt attention, some with their mouths hanging open, and several children were pressed up tight against their mothers' arms with frightened looks in their eyes.

Reverend Redmon raised up his head and shouted, "That's ole Satan underneath the church uh trying to cause trouble." He pounded on the floor. "Come on out of there, you red varmint. Come on out so's we'uns can evict you from our heads evermore." He lunged to his feet and ran to the altar.

By this time, the entire congregation was on their feet, shouting "Amen" and "Hallelujah".

Thorney Dalton rushed down the aisle, stopped in front of the altar, and began stomping his feet, yelling, "Come on outer there, you red rascal, so we'uns kin evict you from our heads forevermore."

The parishioners joined in, chanting, "Come on out, come on out, come on out."

The reverend pressed the pad again and thump, thump, thump boomed through the small church. Everyone got quiet except for a few nervous, hissing whispers.

Beulah Waters from over on Skunk Creek, her arms raised toward the ceiling, beseeching the heavens, tears running down her round, flushed cheeks, shouted, "Hey, Lordie, please help us here and save us'ns from the bad man."

Junior Bull Elliott and Possum Gilliam, never ones to be left out, ran up to the altar. Junior was known for his philosophy of life that any problem, no matter how big or small, could be fixed with violence, and the bigger the problem, the more violence was required. He was a large, strong farmer and this had always worked for him. Possum was a skinny, shifty-eyed young man who always acted nervous and had a high-pitched voice. The mountain people thought he and Bull the most unlikely of friends.

Bull addressed the reverend. "Me and ole Possum here are goin' down under the church and roust out that red varmint." He looked around at the parishioners and continued, "And when we do, I'm a gonna kick his red, skinny butt all the way ter Old Fort."

I didn't think Possum Gilliam, with his eyes darting around and his Adams apple bobbing up and down, seemed as enthusiastic as Bull.

The reverend sent a panicked look to Fletcher who shrugged his shoulders. Everyone, most especially Possum, knew when Bull Elliott got an idea, he was not easily dissuaded and best not get in his way. The two rushed out, and while they were gone, Reverend Redmon did his best to calm down the frenzied congregation while I tried my hardest not to look at my husband. I knew if I did, I would start laughing so hard, I'd probably fall off the bench.

It wasn't long before Bull and Possum were back. Bull said, "We'uns didn't find him but we saw that he had built some kinda contraption down there so we tore it down. I don't reckon he'll bother us no more, not if he got a good look at the two of us." Bull puffed up his barrel chest and Possum tried to do likewise but without much success.

"Well, I thank you boys," Reverend Redmon said with a relieved look, then after everyone was once more seated, continued on with his sermon. No more thumps were heard and it was the general consensus that once the red devil got a good look at Bull and possibly Possum, he reckoned he might be needed elsewhere and lit out from under the church. After the sermon, everyone came up to the altar to tell Reverend Redmon what a great job he did keeping ole Satan out of their heads. A visiting couple from Knoxville said they wished there was a preacher of the reverend's caliber in Tennessee, a compliment the reverend took to heart, seeming to have forgotten the only devil's work at play was his own.

Bull and Possum became a sort of legend by showing their bravery in going under the church to roust Satan out and were not above bragging about this to all the pretty girls. To this day, the only ones aware that the contraption under the church was man's work and not the red devil's were the reverend, Fletcher and myself.

Each Wednesday, the men and women of the church would gather at one or another's home for a weekly prayer meeting, the men meeting in the living room and the women in the kitchen. The children would be delegated to the bedrooms, the younger ones under the supervision of their older brothers and sisters. Nettie Ledbetter, a prominent member of the flock who considered herself the only person capable of overseeing any church function, chose herself to lead the women's prayer group, dispensing remarks guised as helpful comments but most hateful in nature to those attending while reading scripture to prove her point.

The Ledbetters were an old family on Stone Mountain and no one was prouder of that fact than Nettie, although her only rightful claim to the name was not by blood but through marriage. Since my arrival on the mountain, I had begun associating some of the mountain folk with the animals they resembled. I thought Nettie may have been a raven or crow in a prior life, with black, beady eyes that darted here and there, never still, searching for something or someone to peck. Her hair was black, her shoulders hunched as if great wings spread beneath her dress. A pointed nose and pinched lips and a reedy voice only served to confirm her similarity to the black birds. And like those birds that seemed so ill-mannered to me, Nettie could not find peace in her life. She held onto an anger that seemed to boil beneath the surface, waiting for the chance to unleash it as a snake might its venom on an unsuspecting person or animal. She could find no beauty in her world and I often wondered what had happened to this woman to cast a dark pall over her vision and sensibilities.

Several of the women in our prayer group found her intimidating and allowed Nettie her petty remarks and outbreaks with bowed head and tear-stained cheeks. Others chose not to attend prayer group unless they knew Nettie was sick or had gone to Asheville to visit her sister and would not be attending. Like some, I had learned to treat

Nettie with a sense of humor and dismissal, for once Nettie learned of one's weakness, she pecked and pecked until that person was raw and broken.

Nettie's husband Merle usually trailed along behind her, lost in his own thoughts, or perhaps misery. He was a thin, delicate-looking man who appeared more an academic than farmer. He always had a pipe clamped between his lips, one he bit into more than smoked. It was rumored when Merle married Nettie, he had a head full of luxurious blond curls and a sturdy, muscular body. Within a year, he was completely bald and many of the mountain people thought he was not long for this world as he seemed too frail to get about.

A month after George and Sadie joined us, Fletch and I hosted a prayer meeting at our home. The humidity had been especially fierce that day and heat still lingered long after the sun went down. I had opened the front and kitchen doors, hoping to create a cross-breeze, but the air seemed to be laden down with so much clamminess, not even a whisper found the strength to sweep through the cabin.

From the kitchen, I could hear men's voices rumbling in the living room, deep and soothing beneath Nettie's shrill piping. I glanced at the other women, noting we had a small group tonight, likely due to the oppressive heat or perhaps the fact that Nettie was in town. Junior Hall's grandmother Martha sat next to me, breathing heavily through her mouth. She was a large woman with a round belly much like her grandson's and I feared her weight would be the death of her. Next to her sat Sheriff Nanny's sweet wife Melinda, a tiny and delicate looking woman with a surprisingly booming laugh that could be infectious. Emily Murphy sat close by her daughter Sofie Hall. My gaze lingered on Sofie, her eyes fixed on the hazy piece of sky visible through the door. She cradled her baby daughter in her arms, and I was relieved to see that the child seemed more content and not so fussy as in the past when her mother had no desire to deal with her.

I knew that some women were afflicted with depression and anxiety after the birth of a baby, but in my eyes, Sofie seemed doomed to it after her man disappeared one night.

Some said he was hunting and may have tangled with a bobcat or bear and been too hurt to make his way home while others assumed he just didn't want the responsibility of a wife and new baby and headed off to another place. Sofie would sit staring into space, ignoring her baby's cries, and would have to be reminded by Emily to feed the infant and tend to her. At church, Emily had asked me if there was anything I could do to help Sofie, so I brewed up a tincture of St. John's Wort and told Emily to give it to her three times each day along with chewing mint leaves several times a day but, most important, to try to get her outside for a daily walk. I strongly believed in the healing power of God's natural world and felt it played an important part in healing those suffering from depression. Since Sofie held the baby, I hoped this meant the herbs and the increased activity were working. As if sensing my thoughts, she turned her attention to me and gave me a slight smile. The baby stirred and Sofie reached down and stroked her cheek. A good sign.

Girlish squealing from outside drew my attention.

Nettie cut off midsentence. "What in the world?"

I smiled. "That's just Liza and Ruth playing in the creek. It's so hot, I imagine that's not a very bad idea."

Her forehead crinkled. "Liza and Ruth? Two very Biblical names, I'm sure. Why haven't we met them, Bess?"

Although I had approached several of the women of our church, along with our pastor, about clothing for George, Sadie and their girls, I chose not to talk to Nettie about this. She would not see this as charity, but, rather, as a way to help those too lazy to help themselves, as she liked to pontificate.

Before I could formulate an answer, Sadie stepped into the kitchen, laughing and saying, "Miss Bess, come cool off in the creek with me and the girls." The wide smile on her face faded when she saw the women gathered there. "Oh, I'm sorry, Miss Bess, I didn't know you was busy."

I smiled at her. "That's all right, Sadie." I stood and went to her, took her hand. "This is my Bible study group. I'd like you to meet everyone." As I introduced her around, I noted the others smiled and nodded while Nettie studied Sadie with a critical eye.

"Whereabouts are you from?" she asked Sadie once I had finished with the introductions.

Sadie gave me a fearful glance. "We come from South Carolina, ma'am."

"George is our handyman," I put in. "Sadie and her two girls help me with chores around here." I smiled at her. "Lord, I don't know how we ever got along without them, they're such a big help to us."

Nettie's lips barely turned upward.

Sadie's gaze lingered on Nettie for a moment. "Well, I best get back to the girls," she said, giving me a small smile. She nodded at the group. "It was nice meeting you ladies."

I returned to my seat and picked up my Bible.

Nettie turned on me, her face rigid. "Bess, what in the world do you and Fletch think you're doing?"

"I don't follow you."

"A Negro family? Here? With all these Red Shirts running around?"

I gave her a shocked look. "Are you a Red Shirt, Nettie?"

She put her hand to her bosom. "Of course not! Have you heard what they do to the Negroes and the families who are supporting them? Why, it's not safe to even be seen with them."

"We don't support Sadie and George. We pay him to help us with our farm." I leaned back. "He's such a good worker, we're thinking about giving him an acre or two to farm as his own."

Nettie's eyes went wide. "If the Red Shirts get wind of that, there's no telling what they'll do to y'all."

"I don't see that it's any business of theirs what we do here or who we hire. George and Sadie aren't involved in politics, why, I don't even think they vote, so why should the Red Shirts even care that they're here? And besides, Nettie, you know as well as I do what an unchristian bunch of cowards they are, trying to keep control of the State legislature for the past several years under the guise of trying to instigate hatred against the Negroes. They don't have the right to say who gets to vote in this state. And the way I see it, Negroes and women alike should be able to vote just like white men do. I don't think there's any passage in the Bible that says they shouldn't."

Nettie glanced around at the other women, all of whom were busy studying the Bibles in their laps.

I smiled at her. "Is there?"

She rose to her feet. "I think it's best we call an end to this prayer meeting. Bess, you should discuss this with your husband. I'd hate to see something happen to you over a matter like this."

I stood and faced her. "As long as Fletch and I live here, they have a home here, Nettie. If you have a problem with that, then you're not welcome here, prayer meeting or not."

Nettie bustled out of the room, calling for her husband. The other women gave me sympathetic smiles but soon followed. Sofie lingered behind and asked if I'd like to hold her baby. I picked her up in my arms, thinking how small and dainty she was. "She's beautiful, Sofie, just like her mama."

She smiled at that. "I just wanted to thank you, Miss Bessie, for what you did for me. That potion you gave Mama really helped. After Ben left, I felt like I'd fallen into a deep, dark hole, and no matter what I did, I couldn't climb out of it. Not even my baby girl could help."

I squeezed her arm. "You're a strong woman, Sofie, stronger than you know, and you and this little girl are going to be just fine."

Her eyes got teary. "Why'd he do it, Miss Bessie? Why'd he leave me like that?" She looked away. "Mama says he might have got hurt huntin' but he never hunted so I know that didn't happen. And he was acting strange right before he, well, disappeared. I reckon he just didn't love me no more."

I shook my head. "Oh, Sofie, I doubt that had anything to do with it. Some men panic, I think. It may be one day he'll walk back in your life as easy as he left. It'll be up to you whether you want to let him back in."

She thought about that. "Mayhap I won't," she said, her mouth set in a firm line. "Mayhap by then I'll have me another man or just decide I don't need one sniffing around me. Far as I can tell, they ain't much good for nothin' no how."

I had to laugh at that.

Emily stepped into the room. "You ready to go, Sofie?" she asked.

Sofie reached for the baby and I placed her in her mother's arms.

Emily smiled at me. "The other day I found some old clothes of Sofie's from when she was a girl. I'm gonna wash them and bring them here for Sadie's two little ones."

"Oh, Emily, we would appreciate that so much."

"And what Nettie said? That don't count. She's just being her crazy, nosy self. You're doing the right thing here, Bess, the Christian thing."

I nodded, grateful for her support. But after Nettie's outburst, I began to wonder why it bothered her so much we had Negroes on our farm. Did she know anyone associated with the Red Shirts? I decided only time would tell and worrying about it wasn't going to make it better.

CHAPTER FIFTEEN

Fall 1908

Madder than a mule chewing bumble bees.

Once Liza got used to me, she took to trailing along behind me like a devoted dog. I enjoyed showing her how to do things and she, like me, especially liked to go into the woods to gather herbs to dry. As we would walk along, I'd tell her the stories Elisi told me and watch her eyes light up as I am sure my own did as Elisi spoke of her people and their ways.

This morning, we would search for ginseng, an herb that I could sell for extra money. I had my eyes on an organ from Sears & Roebuck and had begun saving for it.

"What are we looking for this time, Miss Bess?" Liza asked.

I looked up at the sky and smiled at the color just beginning to show in the leaves signaling the approach of fall, the perfect time for digging ginseng roots "'Sang, this is a 'sang morning, Liza."

"We're going to sing?"

I laughed. "We can do that, too, but we're looking for Ginseng, or 'sang as my great-grandmother calls it."

"Ginseng, that's a pretty name."

"It is," I agreed. "It isn't always easy to find, but I'll teach you a trick Elisi taught me. When hunting ginseng you need to remember the rule of three. The first rule is to keep your eyes on the ground and watch for two blues and a red."

"Huh?"

"Three types of berries; the bright blue of Blue Cohosh, the dark blue-black of Solomon's Seal, and the one we really want, the red of Ginseng. They tend to grow near each other, Blue Cohosh, Solomon's Seal, and Ginseng."

She nodded. "Blue, blue-black, and red, but we want the red ones."

"Exactly." I held up my basket. "But I wouldn't be averse to having some of the others to add to my medicine cabinet. The second rule is to harvest only from plants that are mature, old enough to give us the roots we want."

"But how do we know until we dig them up?"

"If the plant is old enough, it will have at least three stalks with berries. The third rule is from the Cherokee People; never dig the first or even the second plant, you must always wait for the third one."

"But why, Miss Bessie?"

"It's a way of preserving the plant population, insuring that the plants will be here for many, many more years. A type of protection we offer to the plants in return for the healing they offer to us."

As we wound our way up the mountain, our eyes on the ground, searching for the red berries topping the green leaves of the plant, Liza said, "Tell me a story, Miss Bessie."

I smiled. She reminded me of myself begging Elisi to tell one of her people's legends or my students at school asking for a story. I had, ever since my first year teaching at Cedar Grove, set aside time in the spring to share the ancient legends and myths of various cultures. The children naturally shared the stories with their parents and thankfully not one parent complained. In fact, they seemed to enjoy the stories as much as their children did. "I'll tell you of the spider and the sun, a story my Cherokee great-grandmother told me."

She mock shivered. "I don't like spiders."

"Maybe not but you'll like this one." I stopped beside a downed tree and set my basket on the ground then settled on the trunk to rest a bit, waiting for Liza to join me. "In the beginning, there was no light, only darkness, and the People couldn't see so they kept bumping into each other. Fox said that people on the other side of the world had plenty of light but were greedy and didn't want to share it. Possum went over there to steal a little piece and found the sun hanging in a tree, lighting up that side of the world. So Possum took a small piece of the sun and hid it in the fur of his tail but the heat burned the fur off and that's why possums have bald tails. Buzzard decided to try, so he hid a piece of the sun in his head feathers but it burned them off and that's why buzzards have bald heads. So Grandmother Spider made a clay bowl then spun a web into what we now call the Milky Way." I looked at Liza. "Remember when Fletch showed it to you, up high in the sky?"

She nodded, her eyes wide. "A spider did all that?" she asked in a small voice.

I smiled. "According to the People, she did. She spun this web across the sky all the way to the other side of the world then snatched up the big ball of sun in the clay bowl and took it home to our side of the world. And then the People had light."

Liza eyed me with suspicion. "Is that true?"

"It is if you choose to believe it." I rose to my feet. "Come, little one, I think there may be a patch of ginseng not far from here. You rested enough?"

Liza stood, placing her small hand in mine. We set off again, Liza singing softly, me occasionally joining in, only stopping when we came across the ginseng then digging it up and placing it in the basket I carried. Doing what Elisi told me the Cherokee did, taking only the third one. I had added another ritual to Elisi's routine when I noted the scarcity of ginseng on the mountain. Taking a few of the red berries in my hand, I crushed them, then buried them in the moist soil, sending up a prayer that the seeds inside would germinate and grow.

The sun told me it was nearing noon, so we stopped on top of the mountain and had our lunch, ham and biscuits, hard-boiled eggs, and apples, slaking our thirst with the sweet water from the spring nearby. Afterward, we lay back on the soft, warm grass, studying the clouds in the sky, Liza telling me what they reminded her of. I was so relaxed, I wanted to stay there a bit longer but the sun dropped too fast and I knew if we didn't leave soon, we would be returning in the dark, a time to be inside and away from the nocturnal animals that liked to wander about searching for prey.

Halfway down the mountain, Liza stopped suddenly, her head tilted.

I turned to her. "What is it?"

"Did you hear someone scream?" she said, her eyes wide.

I shook my head. "Maybe you heard a bobcat off in the distance. They sound like a woman screaming, sometimes like a baby crying."

She nodded but quickened her pace as we traveled down the narrow trail. Closer to the house, I heard muffled voices then a woman's piercing shriek.

"Mama," Liza said, breaking into a run.

She was fast for such a small girl and it took some effort to keep up with her. We broke into the clearing behind the house and both stopped at the sight of a group of men, none of whom I recognized, gathered around George, pushing and shoving at him as if herding him toward some unknown destination. George's face was bloody and his shirt torn and he resisted as best he could but even as strong as George was he could not best a group of raving madmen. When I saw one man with a thick rope in his hands, fear clutched at my heart and I stifled my own scream. I searched for Sadie and Ruth and finally found Sadie off to the side of the house, tears streaming down her face as she screamed in terror. She had her arms around her young daughter, whom she had turned so that the little girl's face was hidden in her apron. I started to go to her but she caught sight of me and shook her head, then nodded toward the cabin. I understood immediately. She didn't want Liza to see whatever was going on out here.

I guided Liza up the back porch and into the kitchen, speaking in a low voice, panic slithering up my spine like a poisonous snake. In the house, I knelt before her. "You need to stay in here, Liza, it's what your mama wants."

"But Daddy..."

"I know. I'm going to go out there and see if I can put a

stop to this. But you need to stay here. You may make it worse if you go out there and they see you. So just stay below the window, don't let those men catch sight of you, and let me see what I can do."

I rose, my eyes searching the kitchen for a weapon, wishing Fletcher were here. But he had gone into Old Fort for supplies and wasn't expected back until after dark. When I saw the shotgun leaning against the wall behind the door, relief swept through me. I hurried over to it, picked it up, jacked it open to make sure it was loaded. I dropped extra shotgun shells in my apron pocket and stepped outside.

I hurried across the yard toward the men, who had gotten George close to an old oak tree near the creek bed. A couple saw me but ignored me as if I was no threat to them. They stopped in front of the tree and the man with the rope threw it over the lowest limb as the other men jostled George closer. I stopped, took aim and fired the shotgun at the limb and it split from the tree with a tremendous whacking sound, peppering some of the men with bits of bark. It landed in the middle of the group and the men broke apart, leaving George surrounded, but their attention now focused on me.

"Next one goes to whoever tries to put that rope around his neck," I said, my voice rough.

Some of the men grumbled amongst themselves but one stepped apart. The politician. Of course, I thought. He's come to show us the way of his world. "Mr. Belle," I said, "I think you and your cohorts need to get off my property now before someone gets hurt."

He duck walked closer. "Well, now, we're just here dispensing justice," he said in his high, nasal voice.

"No justice needs to be done here except that you all need to get off my land. I have the right by law to shoot anyone trespassing on my property." I cocked the gun and aimed it at his head. "Go. Now. If you want to live." It took much effort to control my arms so that the gun wouldn't shake with the fear I felt.

"We caught this nigger stealing from your garden," he yelled, pointing that way. "Putting it all in a big ole bushel, he was. Stealing's a hanging offense."

I shook my head with disgust. "This man works for my husband. He wasn't stealing, he was working, and you have no right coming on our land and trying to make trouble for him just because he's of a different color." I studied him for a moment. "Seems mighty suspicious you show up here when Fletcher's in town. It being a workday and all, I'd think you would have your own business to attend to, Mr. Belle, or is your business going around hanging people for no good reason?"

The men behind him moved restlessly but I was relieved to see they no longer saw the need to hold George and that the one with the rope hadn't tried to put it over another limb.

"And all of you men," I shouted, "who apparently have nothing better to do with your time than be persuaded to do another man's evil deed, take heed that this is our hired hand and he has every right to be on this property, doing whatever we ask him to do, and you don't have the right to interfere with that." I shot the gun near Mr. Belle's feet. He jumped a good six inches off the ground and began to back away. "Sheriff Nanny's a good friend of mine and Fletcher's, and he's a Democrat," I continued, loading the gun. I smiled at Mr. Belle. "And I reckon he'd be more than happy to pay a visit to each and every one of you and set you straight on trespassing and trying to take the law into your own hands." I aimed the shotgun at Mr. Belle. "Now, get. Right now before I just can't stand the sight of you anymore and do something about it."

I watched as Mr. Belle duck walked toward the road, the men falling in behind him, some grumbling to each other, some giving me hostile looks, others appearing contrite. Maybe they'd think twice next time they decided to do something so evil but I suspected these men were either dimwitted enough to be swayed by another man's bias or perhaps destitute enough to do anything for a bit of change in their pocket. Either way, they were dangerous and I admit to being glad none of them lived on our mountain.

Sadie and Ruth hurried over to George and I felt the air stir as Liza dashed by me. George put his arms around his wife and daughters, talking in a low voice, trying to soothe their tears. He looked at me and said, "I thank you, ma'am. You saved my life today. I'll owe you for the rest of my life." He swallowed, looking around. "I just pray it don't make things hard for you."

"If they do, they don't know what they're going to be up against if they mess with Fletcher."

George's lips twitched. "Or you, ma'am."

I nodded at his face. "Let's get you inside and see to those cuts."

"Yes, ma'am."

Inside the kitchen, my knees shook so much, I had to lean on the shotgun for a moment. When I heard them coming in behind me, I forced myself to straighten up, put the shotgun beside the door and walk to the cupboard to fetch my dried herbs and rags.

George's injuries were such that he did not require much care other than cleaning and treating scratches and putting a poultice on his bruised face. He sat in the chair, stoic and strong, teasing his two daughters, trying to put them at ease. They quickly warmed to his dramatic faces and fake cries of pain while

Sadie continued to pace the kitchen, wringing her hands while darting glances at her husband. As I was putting away my medicines, she told the girls to go outside and play. Once they were far enough away so as not to be heard, she turned to her husband and said, "We got to leave this place."

I stiffened as shock coursed through my body. I didn't think I could stand losing those two precious girls and this man and woman who had come to mean so much to me. "Sadie," I said but she waved her hand at me and shook her head.

"No, don't try to talk me out of it," she said, tears streaming down her face. "It's dangerous here with them Red Shirts around. I was hoping they'd leave us alone but they ain't going to, Miss Bessie, you know that."

George put his hand on her arm, drew her closer to him. "Don't fret so, Sadie. We're happy here. Why, you say so yourself all the time. Those men won't be back, not after what happened."

Sadie's eyes were wild with panic. "They'll be more determined than ever to get you. Miss Bessie done humiliated them, they'll want revenge."

A chill spread throughout my body. Was she right? Would they feel the need to avenge themselves? But what else could I have done? "Sadie, I couldn't let them hang George, you know that."

"'Course not, Miss Bessie, and I thank you for saving him but it'd be better if we just left." She turned to her husband. "We can go to Virginia, like we talked about when we first set out, live with my brother till we get on our feet. He says it's safer up there, ain't so many Red Shirts and Ku Klux Klans around."

George shook his head. "I ain't going, Sadie. Mr. Fletch's done give me two acres to farm as my own. I ain't never had nothin' in my life till I came here. We got us a home here, food in our bellies, our girls are healthy and growing strong. 'Sides, Miss Bessie's teaching them their letters and numbers so they'll be good and educated when they're grown." His eyes locked with her. "They'll have a better life than us 'cause they'll know how to read and write and I mean to see to it that they don't want for nothin'."

I stepped closer to her. "Sadie, I promise you Fletcher and I will do everything we can to keep you all safe. You're part of our family now, we love you all."

Sadie's face fell. "We need to go," she said in a small voice. "It ain't safe here no more." She gazed into her husband's eyes for several long moments then sighed with defeat. "Well, if you won't go then I guess I won't either, George, but I got a bad feeling about this."

George smiled and pulled her into his arms. "We'll be fine, Sadie, we're right where we're supposed to be."

I smiled with relief and vowed to myself Fletch and I would see to it that this sweet family came to no harm.

When Fletcher returned and learned what happened to George, he threatened to track down the Red Shirt politician and put an end to his threats. George and I managed to talk him out of it but only after Fletcher elicited a promise from George that he would not leave our property unless he was with Fletcher and would keep a rifle nearby when he was working in the fields or on the mountain. I didn't think the men would harm Sadie or her girls but was determined to keep them in sight at all times. And as I watched George cross the creek and go up the steps to his cabin, I sensed a dark pall surrounding him but told myself it was only because of what had happened.

That would be the last time I would ignore my sight which at times seemed more curse than gift.

CHAPTER SIXTEEN

Fall 1908

Finer than frog hair split four ways.

It was a beautiful evening with a cool breeze blowing down off the mountain bringing the fresh scent of pine, a perfect time to snap green beans on the front porch. Fletch and George had gone off tracking a bobcat that had gotten into the chicken coop the past two nights and I could hear Sadie's soft voice across the way singing a soothing lullaby to her two girls. Once they were down, I could count on her to join me and help with my chore but for now everything was peaceful and I couldn't help but think how beautiful our world was as I looked out at the mountains surrounding me, the sky a rosy color as the sun began its dip behind the ridges.

A horse neighed and I glanced up to see the sheriff's tall sorrel cantering down our dirt path. Sheriff Nanny always put me in mind of his two eccentric cousins, Doc and Horace, who lived in Hot Springs. I hoped one day they would join the rest of their family in Old Fort. The town could use a gifted musician like Doc and I missed watching Horace parade around with a bright-colored turban on his head. I watched the sheriff dismount, nodding my head at his greeting.

"Mind if I sit a spell?" he asked, taking off his hat and slapping it against his britches.

"I'd be happy for the company." I motioned for him to

step onto the porch.

He sat in the chair Fletch usually occupied, leaning back on its two hind legs, resting his hat on his knee. "You sure do have a pretty view here, Miss Bessie," he said with appreciation.

I smiled. "Hard to stay off the front porch looking at it."

He nodded. "Fletch close by?"

I shook my head. "He's out tracking a bobcat that keeps getting into the chickens."

"He see it get into the coop?"

"No but the tracks told the tale."

Sheriff Nanny shook his head. "Strangest tracks you'll ever find. Looks like a two-legged animal you're trailing, the way they place their back paws right where their front paws were."

"I hope he finds the varmint. We're losing too many chickens."

Sheriff Nanny settled back, rocking in the chair for a few minutes while I snapped my beans. After a bit, he said, "I hear you had a run-in with some Red Shirts."

I glanced at him. So this must be an official visit.

He smiled. "Heard you put them in their place. Mighty brave thing for you to do and I've come to thank you for that."

"They were nothing but a mob looking for any reason to lynch a colored man and thought they found one here. What they didn't know was I'm a teacher and I've dealt with meaner bullies than them. They thought I'd let them do whatever they wanted to."

Sheriff Nanny grinned. "Till you took the shotgun to 'em."

"Had to stop it. I couldn't let them hang an innocent man much less Fletcher's help."

Sheriff Nanny shook his head. "I'll tell you true, Miss Bessie, that Orson Belle is a pain in my backside, and he ain't even from around here. He usually stays over to Old Fort way but the times he makes it over to our mountain, you can bet he's up to no good. Don't know how in the world he manages to keep getting himself on the ticket for legislator. But it seems that fool Furnifold Simmons has a lot of power in this state. He's peppering the whole of western North Carolina with his Red Shirts, hoping to keep control of the State Legislature from the Republicans and keep the coloreds out of politics."

"Way I see it, they have as much right to be there as we do, Sheriff."

"I agree with that, but there ain't no talking to an idiot who thinks he's got the right of it and everybody else is wrong." He shook his head. "I swear, ain't nothing worse than a religious zealot or power-mad politician."

I smiled. "Well, loading a shotgun with buckshot does get their attention."

He laughed a hearty laugh, running his hands through his hair. Those hands reminded me of Theodore Norton, Papa's deputy back in Hot Springs, who had huge, powerful hands that could be as gentle as a kitten or as hard as an iron skillet, I'd heard tell. Papa's last letter delivered the sad news that Mr. Norton had been shot dead in the street by a jealous husband. Mr. Norton's flirtatious ways had finally caught up with him and grief pierced my heart at the thought of this. The sheriff cleared his throat, turning my attention to him.

"I don't reckon you need worry yourself too much about them Red Shirts, Bess. The KKK don't like competition and I reckon their leader Horace Gilliam..." He winked. "They call him the Grand Wizard, and for the life of me I don't see nothing about the KKK or old Horace that has to do with a wizard. Anyway, once he hears what they've been up to, he'll let them know soon enough they're not welcome here." He glanced at me. "I don't abide by their politics, but since Horace took over, they've calmed down a bit. I reckon it's more to do with the fact that ole Horace is a lazy son of a gun who would rather be in his bed come nightfall than out burning crosses or harassing poor souls." He shook his head and chuckled.

I gave him a curious look.

He grinned. "I was just thinking about a story I heard from Horace's wife about their nephew Possum and Uncle Willie Moffitt's wake."

"The old man who gave everyone nicknames? I was sorry to hear of his passing."

"Ol' buggar went the best way, died in his sleep."

We were silent a moment, each remembering the colorful old man who liked to tell humorous stories about his friends and neighbors but most especially himself. I didn't know him personally but had heard a lot of stories about him.

Sheriff Nanny crossed an ankle over his knee. "I reckon I've seen y'all at the Stone Mountain Baptist Church. With my job, I don't get much time for church-going but I try to attend as much as I can. Anyway, Reverend Redmon took charge of the arrangements after Uncle Willie died. He had the old man dressed in his finest clothes then propped him up on his bed so everyone could come and pay their respects. Why, people came from all around with food and everyone had a fine time talking about what a fine old man he was. By the end of the day, it started to rain and most of the neighbors had gone home. Reverend Redmon wanted to go home, too, but he didn't think it proper to leave Willie alone all night even though the old man had lived by himself for years. He talked this over with Bull Elliott and his friend Possum Gilliam..." he paused. "Being parishioners of Stone Mountain Baptist Church, I reckon you know them."

I smiled. "They're quite a pair, aren't they?" These two were not known for their intelligence and seemed to always be in some sort of plight together.

"Well, there was still a lot of food left over and Bull took one look at all that good food and thought it'd be a good idea for him and Possum to stay with the old man through the night. Possum was a bit scared at the thought but he knew better than to disagree with Bull 'cause, as the whole mountain knows, Bull always gets his way and there ain't no use arguing about it. After the reverend left, Bull and Possum ate till they were about to bust then Bull went outside to fetch a bottle of Thorney Dalton's white lightning, a particular blend I'm told he calls Hurricane Juice because it comes on fast and furious. After the boys got a few drinks in them, they decided to prop Uncle Willie in a chair beside the fireplace. They stood back admiring the way he looked, thinking that with the firelight reflecting off his face, he appeared to be sleeping. By that time, Bull was pretty drunk and started telling Uncle Willie funny stories about his adventures with Possum and the pretty girls over in Old Fort. Possum, being more of a silent drunk than Bull, pulled up a chair beside Uncle Willie while Bull poured whiskey in a glass then tied it to the old man's hand with a handkerchief so it looked like he had passed out after drinking. Bull thought this was awful funny but Possum, who by this time had forgotten the old man was dead, kept explaining to Uncle Willie that Bull wasn't making fun of him, he was just having fun."

I laughed at this image, the green beans in my lap by now forgotten.

"Well, around about midnight, they heard someone outside so Bull went out to see who had come to visit. Possum heard Bull shout, 'Y'all come on in here, we got us a party going,' and watched as 'Bad-eye' Bruce Hudgins and Cotton and Goober Davis came into the house. Now, I don't know if you've seen Cotton and Goober, but Cotton has a large, round face and bulging eyes, and Goober's always turning his head sideways and squinting one eye closed when he talks. And the two of them's always fighting over something or other but they're always together. When Cotton asked what Bull and Possum were doing at Uncle Willie's, Bull realized they hadn't heard Uncle Willie had died so he decided to have some fun with them and told them he and Possum were having a party with the old man. Cotton looked at Uncle Willie and wanted to know why he was all dressed up and Bull told him he was gonna have a big day the next day and was going on a long trip.

"Now, Possum and Bad-eye Bruce were enemies through school and never liked one another. When Bad-eye went close to the old man, Possum stepped between the two and told him the old man was sleeping and to leave him alone so Bad-eye joined the Cotton brothers eating the leftover food. After some more drinking, Bull and the Davis brothers started scuffling with one another but Bad-eye couldn't take his eyes off the old man. He said, 'He looks dead to me, how much juice did the old buggar drink?' Possum, who always took the opposite side from Bad-eye, that being the way of natural enemies, told him the old man was sleeping and to leave him alone. Goober pushed his brother against the fireplace and Cotton fell on the floor beside Uncle Willie's chair, causing the glass of whiskey in the old man's hand to drop, splashing on Cotton's face and chest, then breaking on the rock fireplace, scattering glass all over the floor. Cotton looked up at Uncle Willie and thought he saw the old man grinning. He flew into a rage, jumped up and shoved Uncle Willie and his chair across the floor. The old man went flying and came to rest against the table with his head and neck at an unnatural angle.

"Bull ran over to Uncle Willie and checked his pulse, saying, 'He's dead,' while shaking his head. Possum was devastated at this news and shouted at Cotton, 'You done kilt him again, why'd you do that? He was the best ol' feller in the whole county and now look at him. You even got his suit dirty.'"

I laughed so hard at this, I had to wipe tears from my eyes.

Sheriff Nanny waited on me before continuing. "Bull shook his head and said, 'I guess we getter go git the sheriff on this. He'll want to investigate.'

"Cotton was horrified at this news. He and I have had some unpleasant meet-ups in the past and I reckon he didn't want to face another one. He said, 'Now wait a minute. I got somethin' to say before you goes off to get the shurf. I pushed the ol man, alright, I admit that, but it was self-defense. He pulled a knife on me.'"

Sheriff Nanny looked at me and we both burst out laughing. We were still laughing when Fletch and George joined us and I got to hear the story all over again. It was times like this when I felt a part of this community of mountain people whose ways seemed so strange and eccentric to me at times.

CHAPTER SEVENTEEN

Spring 1909

You better give your heart to Jesus, 'cause your butt is mine.

That winter was a particularly fierce one and we saw no more of the Red Shirts. I wasn't sure if it was because of the frigid weather or if Horace Gilliam had done what Sheriff Nanny thought he would and run them off. I prayed the little politician had waddled back to wherever he came from and would leave the mountain folks alone.

Spring took its sweet time coming to our mountain but when it did we were greeted with spectacular color as the cedars and pines shook off their snowy coats to reveal deep green foliage, with bright yellow Bellwort, the yellowish-green bells of Corn Lilies, deep purple Myrtle and wild violets sprouting from the unfrozen ground, and the redbud trees showing off splendid pink blooms, complementing the dogwood's white flowers in the shape of the cross.

In late spring, as Liza and I made our way up the mountain, searching for wild blackberry bushes, she took my hand and said, "Tell me a story, Miss Bessie."

I smiled, thinking how much I had come to love this precious child with her quick intelligence and unlimited curiosity. "All right. I'll tell you the story of the turtle calendar."

She squinted her eyes at me. "A turtle what?"

I realized she might have no idea what the word *calendar* meant, had probably never set eyes on one. How I wished Liza could attend school but there were none that accepted Negroes back then on Stone Mountain. "A turtle calendar. A calendar is a way to tell the passage of time. You know the concept, Liza. Seven days in a week, four weeks in a month, twelve months in a year?"

She nodded. "Mama taught me the months last year." She smiled at me. "I was born in October. Mama said that's a right good month for a birthday."

I grinned. "Yes, it is. Right when summer's given over to fall. Why, I think you have the prettiest month of the year for a birthday, Liza. The mountains are filled with bright colors, all the trees celebrating your birth by putting on their prettiest finery."

She giggled at that but I could tell the thought pleased her. Her expression sobered. "Did the turtle make the calendar?"

"No, not really, but it relates to our calendar. This happened long ago, before there were People, when all the creatures of the animal kingdom held dominion over the land, sky and waters. A time when all the animals could talk and communicate with one another much like we humans do today."

Her eyes grew wide. "Wouldn't it be something wonderful if we could talk to the animals, Miss Bessie?"

I smiled and squeezed her little hand. "I believe at one time the People were able to do just that, Liza. I wish that were so and fear the fault lies more with humans than the animals. In this time, Turtle was walking across a hillside one day." I winked at her. "As you know, little one, turtles are slow creatures and never seem to travel very far."

Liza nodded. "Ever' time I come across one, it goes into its shell and don't move. Why is that, Miss Bessie?"

"Because that's their way of protecting themselves from people and other animals that might hurt them. They don't know what a sweet child you are and that you would never do them any harm."

Liza shook her head, a solemn look on her face. "Oh, I would never hurt them. I just want to play with them."

"Yes, but they don't know that because they don't understand our language. On that day, Wohali the eagle was soaring high in the sky and with his keen eyes saw Turtle far down below. He flew down and landed on a limb above Turtle so he could speak with his brother. When Turtle saw Eagle, he drew his head into his shell, afraid Eagle was going to eat him.

"'Come out of your shell, Turtle,' said Eagle. 'I come as a friend.'

"Turtle stuck his head out of his shell and asked Eagle what he wanted.

"'I only want to be your friend. I saw you crawling from high above and wondered how far you have traveled in your life.'

"'Not far,' said Turtle. 'I'm very slow and the ground is filled with stones and sticks.'

"Eagle landed in front of Turtle. 'Climb up on my back and hold on tightly and I'll show you the world as you have never seen it.' Turtle cautiously climbed up Eagle's wing and onto his feathered back. 'Hold on tight,' Eagle said and flew off into the sky.

"As they climbed higher and higher, Turtle saw all the distance he had ever traveled in his whole life and all he could have traveled if he crawled along the rest of his life. He was so amazed he forgot he was holding on and let go of Eagle's feathers and down he fell off Eagle's back. Eagle tried hard to catch Turtle but was unable to, and when Turtle hit the Earth, his shell shattered into many ragged pieces. A grew sorrow came over Eagle when he landed beside his new friend for he knew that he had caused Turtle a great injury.

"The Eagle, being the most spiritual of all creatures, began to pray to the Creator for the strength and wisdom to help his friend. As soon as he asked, many animals began to pour out of the woods to the place where Turtle lay dying. Beavers with their sharp teeth came along with squirrels, opossum, raccoons and more and more. Some began to gather pine tar and others ground charcoal so they could make tar pitch. The animals that could began to shape the broken shell pieces with their teeth and slowly Turtle's shell began to take the shape that we know today for all turtles over the Earth Mother. Turtle was saved and the Creator gave his shell a purpose of all things and assembled by all the creatures. Today all descendents of the one Turtle have 13 large spaces on their back with 28 smaller spaces ringing the outside of their shell. This is a calendar which equals 364 days. It never changes and is easily found in the forest on Turtle's back."

I stopped and turned to her. "Do you know how many days there are in a year, Liza?"

She stood there, her forehead wrinkled in concentration. "Mama told me but I don't reckon I recollect."

"There are 365 days in a year, little one."

She pondered this a moment. "But the Turtle Calendar ain't the same as our calendar if it's 364 days, Miss Bessie."

"But there's a reason. Since the beginning of time, the People have a day called the Green Corn. This usually takes place in midsummer when the corn crop is young, green and growing with the promise of another year's bountiful harvest. On this day, great feasts are prepared and all grudges are forgiven. The Black Drink is consumed and everything is given away. But this day does not count as a day because everything starts anew. And that accounts for the 365th day in our calendar. So from now on, when you see Brother Turtle crossing a road, remember what he is, and if you can, stop and give him a little help just like the Eagle did long ago."

Liza looked at me, her gaze solemn. "I will, Miss Bessie. I promise."

I smiled at her. "I know you will, Liza. You're a special child."

We spent most of the morning on the mountain, filling our baskets with blackberries, and when we returned to the cabin, found Fletcher's cousin Boy Elliott sitting on the front porch, a wad of tobacco stuffed in one cheek. When he saw me, he half-rose from his seat, nodding his head. "Mornin' to you, Moonfixer. And who's this pretty little thing you got with you?"

Beside me, Liza beamed with pride. "This is Liza, Boy." I turned to her. "Liza, I'd like you to meet Boy Elliott, he's Mr. Fletch's cousin."

"Right nice to meet you, young lady," Boy said.

Liza gave him a shy smile. "Same here, Mr. Elliott." She studied him for a moment. "How come they call you Boy? Is that your true name?"

Boy shrugged. "I reckon it's the only name I got. My ma and pa died when I was just a little boy, leaving me an orphan. I was too young to know what my real name was so everybody started calling me Boy and I reckon it stuck."

"I reckon it's as good a name as any," Liza said. She turned when her mother hailed her from the front porch of their cabin and gave her a wave. Sadie was heavy with child and depended on her girls to help her around the cabin. "I guess I better go help Mama with the chores, Miss Bessie," she said. "Remember you promised I could help you make a blackberry cobbler this afternoon."

"I won't start without you," I told her and watched as she ran across the field to their cabin.

Boy spat a stream of tobacco off the side of the porch and eased himself back into the chair. I didn't miss his grimace of pain as he settled himself.

I sat the baskets filled with blackberries down beside the door. "What's the matter, Boy, did you get hurt?"

"Reckon I did. I was hoping you could take a look at it and put some of that healing salve you have on it."

"Well, let's have a look."

He raised his pant leg above his boot and showed me a deep gash in the side of his calf. I knelt down and examined it for a moment, debating whether it needed stitches. "When did this happen?"

"Last night or most likely early this morning."

"It's stopped bleeding so we won't need stitches but that needs to be cleaned and treated, Boy. You wait right here and I'll get my supplies."

When I returned, Boy had neatly rolled up his pants to the knee and was stuffing more tobacco in his mouth. "Just in case I need somethin' to chomp down on," he explained.

I pulled my chair close to his and dipped a rag into a bucket of clean water I'd brought with me. When I touched the flesh around the gash, he tensed and a small hiss escaped his lips. "I'm sorry to say this is likely to hurt but this needs to be cleaned. I see debris inside the wound. What'd you gash yourself with?"

"Oh, I managed to run into a broken limb atop a log laying on the ground. Didn't see it in the dark. A-course, I was running helter-skelter and not paying much attention to what was in my path."

I glanced up at him.

He gave me an embarrassed smile. "You believe in haints, Miss Bessie?"

I pulled out a small twig, buried deep in the wound, ignoring his groan, as I thought of all the nights I'd heard the slaves traveling up the trail beside our cabin on their way in from the fields, the quiet shuffling of their feet, the musical clinking of their chains, the soulful songs they sang. But all I said was, "Yes, I do believe in ghosts, Boy." I raised up to look him in the eye. "Why? Did you see one?"

He nodded. "Just last night. And more'n one."

I raised my eyebrows as I applied a decoction of crushed roots of Yellow Dock over the wound to disinfect it. "What happened?"

"Well, I'd been over to the other side of the mountain courtin' this girl I met in Old Fort and it started raining so hard I couldn't see where I was goin'. I just happened to be near Stone Mountain Church so stepped in there to wait out the rain." He hesitated.

I straightened up and looked at him. "Go on."

"Well, I sat down in the back pew there, you know, just listening to the rain, hoping it'd quit soon so I could get home and get me on some dry clothes. It was dark in there but light enough I could see clear to the front of the church." He took time to spit tobacco off the porch. "And when I looked up front, I saw all my dead kin folk just lined up side by side lookin' back at me."

I wondered how I would react if I saw Mama, little Green and Druanna standing in front of me. "I imagine that was a frightful sight, Boy. What'd you do then?"

"I lit on out of there as quick as I could. That's how I hurt my leg. I was runnin' so fast and it was raining so hard, I couldn't hardly see and that ol' log just jabbed me, I guess."

"Did the ghosts say anything to you?"

He glanced away. "I don't reckon I give 'em a chance to, I was so scared."

"I would be, too." I busied myself, soaking a rag in a decoction of tobacco roots, then wrapping it around Boy's calf to aid with the swelling and inflammation.

I smiled as his sigh told me my efforts were giving him some relief. He remained quiet for a bit, watching as I tidied up my mess, and finally said. "You believe me, don't you, Bessie?"

I stared into his eyes. "Why wouldn't I? I'll tell you one thing. You won't catch me alone on this mountain after dark."

He grinned. "I knew if anybody would understand, it'd be you. You got the sight, don't tell me you don't."

"It seems to run in my family," I admitted.

"That's what Fletch says. I reckon he's like most of us Elliotts, ain't never had reason to believe in that sort of thing, but after last night, I shore won't be so quick to make fun of stories of ghosts and haints." He rose to his feet, gingerly putting weight on his injured leg. "I reckon that'll do," he said, shooting me a smile. He stuffed his hat back on his head. "I best get on home now and see to my chores. I thank you for your doctoring, Bess. I left you a crock of butter inside the kitchen there."

"You didn't have to do that but I do thank you, Boy." I stood on the porch, watching him limp away down the path, stopping every now and then to spit tobacco juice to the side, hoping he would do as I had advised, keep the wound clean and change the bandage daily, knowing he probably wouldn't. These mountain men were hardy and virile and thought themselves indispensible from something as minor as a cut. But I knew infection could be a deadly enemy and fell the strongest of men. Just look what it did to Mr. Solomon.

I went inside and loaded a picnic basket with biscuits, fried chicken, and stewed apples and carried it to the creek, calling for Sadie and her girls. All three came and stood in the doorway, Sadie holding her hands under her swollen belly as if to support it. "I fixed lunch. Let's have a picnic by the creek," I said.

Liza and Ruth whooped with joy, darting off the porch and running to join me. I spread an old quilt along the grassy bank and we enjoyed a lazy meal filled with laughter and talk. I could tell the pregnancy was taking its toll on Sadie. She looked tired and couldn't seem to get comfortable. When I asked if there was anything I could to help her, she gave me her shy smile and said, "I reckon you done more than enough for us, Miss Bessie." Tears gathered in her eyes. "Why, I don't know that I've ever been this happy afore. We got us a nice home here with you nice folks. George loves working for Mr. Fletch and gettin' to farm his own garden. My girls are learning to read, somethin' I always wanted for them, and I thank you for that."

"I can teach you too, Sadie."

"I want you to after my boy's born." She rubbed her belly.

"You think it's a boy?"

She smiled. "Oh, I know it's a boy. This one's different."

We watched the girls playing in the creek, splashing one another and dancing around, their laughter ringing off the mountainside, and I wished I could hold this moment for a long time, the joy of life now and the promise of life to come. But when I looked at Sadie, I saw darkness there, and I worried she would not survive her baby's birth, or the baby wouldn't, and so I could not let go of this and the brightness of the day seemed to dim.

After a bit, Sadie called her girls to her and they went inside for an afternoon nap. I fetched a book from inside our cabin and sat on the porch reading, our barn cat purring on my lap.

The jangle of a horse's reins caught my attention and I looked up. Two men on horseback rode down the path to our house. Fear spiked my brain when I noticed the red bandanas over their faces matching their bright red shirts. Something bounced along behind one of the horses but I couldn't make it out between the horse's legs. The men stopped at the edge of the path and one threw down a rope. I got to my feet, wishing Fletcher hadn't taken the shotgun with him when he left that morning.

"We brought you somethin'," the man called. Before I could respond, he wheeled his horse around and trotted off at a fast pace.

I stared at that dark red bundle on the ground, my brain refusing to register what my eyes saw. And when I heard him groan, I jammed my fist into my mouth so Sadie would not hear me scream and ran to him.

CHAPTER EIGHTEEN

Spring 1909

Old devils never die.

The copper smell of blood was so strong, I imagined I could taste it as I knelt beside the body. There was so much blood, I at first wasn't sure who the man was. Most of the clothes had been torn away and what body part wasn't colored red was covered with dirt and mud. Please, God, don't let this be Fetcher, I prayed, as I gingerly turned him over and stared into soulful brown eyes.

"Oh, George," I said, tears falling down my face. "What did they do to you?"

He tried to speak but couldn't. I put my hand on his lips. "Shhh. We'll take care of you, George. I know you have to be hurting something awful but I'll make you feel better, I promise." I looked around anxiously. Where was Fletcher? He should have been back by now. I wanted to touch George's body, to comfort him, cover him, but was terrified I'd cause him more pain.

George wrapped his hand around my wrist and I was surprised at the strength. How is he able to move, having lost all this blood, I wondered wildly.

He tried to raise his head but managed to lift it only a fraction of an inch. When he spoke, his voice was low and rough and filled with pain. "Promise me you and Mr. Fletch will take care of my family, Miss Bessie."

I nodded. "Till you're better. You wait here, George. I'll go get something to give you for the pain then we'll get you in the house…"

"Take care of them," he insisted.

"I will, George. I love them like my own."

He gritted his teeth before continuing. "Don't let them monsters get my babies."

"I'll kill them first, George. If I could, I'd kill whoever did this to you right now, without even thinking about it."

I heard a horse behind me and looked around, thinking if it was those Red Shirts, I'd yank them down off those horses and hit them with my fists until they were dead. Relief flowed through me at the sight of Fletch. He reined up beside us, jumped off his horse, and knelt beside George. "Friend," he said to him, and I burst into tears.

Fletcher reached over and touched my arm. My eyes met his and I shook my head. George would not live. Not with a body so broken and torn and covered with all that blood.

I watched Fletcher's eyes harden, saw the hatred come into them, and knew he saw the same in my own.

George tightened his grip on my arm. "Remember your promise," he said and I watched as his soul left his body.

"Dammit. I'll kill those sons of bitches," Fletcher said, lurching to his feet and walking away. He stood with his back to me for awhile and I left him to grieve. I took my apron off and put it over George's face, looked up to the heavens and asked God why he had to take the good ones, it was always the good ones. Green, Mama, Druanna, little Mark, Fletcher's pa, and now George. How many deaths would I see in my lifetime, I wondered.

Fletcher returned to my side and knelt beside me. His eyes were red and when he spoke his voice was raspy. "We've got to get him in the barn before the girls see him, Bess. They don't need to see their Pa like this."

I nodded. "I'll go get a quilt to cover him." I ran to the house, tears streaming down my face, thinking how in the world am I going to tell Sadie her man's dead? Then remembered our conversation by the creek and I had to bite my cheek to keep from screaming out loud, cursing God and this hateful world. It was not right that a man had to die simply because of the color of his skin. Those evil men who did this to him should be dead, not dear, sweet George.

We covered George with the quilt, wrapping it tight around him. George was such a large man, it took both of us to carry him to the barn. We were almost there when the quilt came partially undone, baring his face. We lay George's body down to rewrap it and I heard a loud screech behind me. I looked up and there stood Sadie, staring at her husband's broken body, her two young girls clinging to her skirts. Sadie collapsed in the yard, screaming with agony. Liza and Ruth held tight to their mother, tears streaming down their faces, making pitiful sobbing sounds. Sadie clutched her swollen belly, doubling over, and panic stuttered up my spine when I saw the dirt beneath her change to mud.

"Her water broke," I told Fletch as I rushed toward her. He helped peel the girls off Sadie then picked her up in his arms. "Our cabin," I told him, clutching each girl by their hand and taking them with me. We rushed into the kitchen and I pulled them into a quick embrace as Fletcher passed us, carrying Sadie to our bedroom. "We have to help your mama," I told them. "She's having her baby." I bent down so our eyes were level. "I know you're hurting over your pa but do you think you can help me until the midwife gets here?"

Each girl gave me a solemn nod, wiping at their eyes, sniffling their noses. "Liza, pour water from that bucket over there into the big pot on top of the stove and set it to boiling. Ruthie, gather up clean rags and bring them into the bedroom. I need you to stay inside, now. You don't need to go out there." As I put on another apron, I watched them scurry off then rushed into the room where Sadie lay doubled up on the bed, moaning. Fletch stood nearby, wringing his hat in his hand, watching her with a worried frown. When our eyes met, I said, "Go fetch Miss Ellie, Fletch. I've never birthed a baby before, not by myself."

With a look of relief, he nodded. "I'll put George in the barn first," he said as he left.

I placed my hands on Sadie's shoulder, turned her toward me and wiped her face with my apron. "Sadie, I know you're grieving but your baby's coming and I need you to concentrate on that now. Can you do that, honey? Can you focus on your baby?"

She made a determined effort to get herself under control. As I watched her, I wondered if I would be able to do the same if anything happened to Fletch. It was all so sad and unnecessary, I thought, and anger spiked my brain that something this horrible had to happen to this sweet woman and her two little girls.

Sadie gasped and clutched her stomach, drawing up her legs. "My back feels like it's gonna split in two, Miss Bessie," she grunted. "I ain't never had this kind of pain afore."

I felt so helpless. I'd watched Mama go through labor but she had seemed to sail right through it, happy at the thought that a baby was coming. "We'll get through this, Sadie, don't you worry about that. It may be this one's a bigger baby and he's needing more room than your girls did."

A flash of light brightened her pain-filled eyes. "You think it's a boy, too, Miss Bessie? I told George we was gonna have us a boy just like... Oh, why did that have to happen to my man," she screamed, turning on her side.

"It's not right, Sadie, and I promise you Fletcher and I will do what we can to make it right." I rubbed her back, waiting for the contraction to pass.

Liza and Ruth came into the room, their eyes on their mother, wide with alarm. "Girls, this is a natural thing," I told them. "So don't worry about your mama. I'm gonna take care of her just fine. Liza, why don't you take Ruth into the kitchen and start washing those blackberries for me? Once your mama has this baby, we'll make us a cobbler because she's going to be so hungry." I tried to instill confidence and lightness in my voice but sensed I failed miserably.

Liza nodded at me as she took her sister's hand. I remembered George's body in the barn and called out as they left the room, "Remember, don't go outside, now, you stay in the kitchen where I can hear you and you can hear me if I need your help."

"Yes, ma'am," they said in small voices.

Sadie rolled onto her back, her face bathed in sweat. I dipped a clean rag into the wash basin and washed her off, talking to her in low, soothing tones. She didn't seem to hear me as she gazed off in the distance, crying in silence.

And so the hours passed, Sadie screeching with pain with each contraction and me worrying where Fletch was and why hadn't he fetched the midwife yet. And what would I do if the baby came before they got here? Well, I'd watched Mama birth Jack, I told myself, I reckoned I could deliver this baby. But something was wrong; I sensed it in the way the labor progressed, the horrible pain Sadie endured with each contraction which seemed to go on and on with no urge to push.

Finally I heard footsteps come into the house and glanced up when Fletch guided Miss Ellie into the room. She was so old no one could guess her age anymore; her white hair so thin you could see her scalp, her back bowed by the years, her wizened face peering up from beneath her shoulders like a turtle coming out of its shell. "How long's she been like this?" she asked without any preamble.

"Since right before Fletch left. That was how long ago?" I darted a look outside, startled to see deep shadows in the yard.

"I been gone at least four hours." He looked at me. "I had to track Miss Ellie down, she was over at the Weavers' helping with their new baby girl." His eyes darted to Miss Ellie, bending over Sadie, and then returned to me. I could see he was embarrassed. "I need to go outside and see to..."

I nodded. "Check on the girls for me before you go, Fletch. Make sure you tell them to stay inside."

Fletch nodded before stuffing his hat back on his head and heading out.

It was a long night filled with screams of pain, frantic whispers and hurried movements. Fletcher fed Liza and Ruth dinner then took the two girls to their cabin and spent the night with them there. I tried Elisi's trick of giving Sadie a piece of leather to clamp down on during the contractions but her pain was such that she could only scream and pray for release.

Finally, Miss Ellie turned to me, a concerned frown on her wrinkled face. "The baby's turned the wrong way," she whispered, "that's why it's taking so long. We got to get it turned around afore it kills her or the baby." She had Sadie get on all fours like an animal then I watched as Miss Ellie put her hands inside and tried to rotate the baby. Sadie screamed and screamed and I thought I would go mad. Finally Miss Ellie withdrew her hands and gave me a curt nod. Within minutes, Sadie started pushing and with a great gush of fluid a baby boy slid into Miss Ellie's arms. I smiled with delight until I noticed the infant's bluish hue and that he was so very still. He didn't cry as I expected him to and I moved closer to Miss Ellie to see what was wrong.

Sadie raised her head. "What's wrong? Why ain't my baby crying?" Her voice rose with panic.

I looked at the small baby boy in Miss Ellie's arms, at the umbilical cord wrapped around his neck, which must have tightened during the birth and strangled him. I closed my eyes and put my fist to my mouth, trying not to let Sadie see my distress.

"Is he all right?" she said, her voice small.

Miss Ellie handed the child to me. "I'll clean her up, you take care of the baby."

I held the small infant in my arms, wondering how a sweet, merciful God could take first the husband then the baby within a day's time. I turned to Sadie. "Let me clean him up for you, then you can hold him."

"But why ain't he crying?" she asked with a panicked look.

I didn't answer as I took a clean rag and wiped him off, marveling at his perfect little body.

"Why won't you talk to me?" Sadie said, her voice shrill.

I walked over to the bed and placed him in his mother's arms. "I'm so sorry, Sadie."

I cried with her as she held her baby close and rocked him, saying, "No, no, no."

I could not bear to watch Sadie grieve so instead focused on Miss Ellie and what she did for Sadie after the delivery, telling myself I needed to know these things. And when Miss Ellie had gathered up the stained linen and bustled out, I turned my attention back to Sadie, now lying on her side, the baby bundled against her. "Can I see him, Sadie?"

She nodded, pulling aside the blanket she had tucked around him.

"Oh," I said, in awe, staring at his skin the color George's had been, with black, curly hair and perfect dark arches above his eyes. "He's perfect, Sadie. Just beautiful. He looks just like his..." I couldn't hold my tears any longer and squeezed her hand before rushing out of the room.

I ran to the barn, hoping to find time alone so I could get myself under control. Instead, I found Fletcher working on George's coffin. He looked up when I stumbled through the door. "Bess?" he said, coming to me and gathering me in his arms.

"He died, Fletch, the baby died."

"Oh, no," he groaned. He held me tight until I had cried myself out. I told him what happened, wondering if the baby would have lived if Miss Ellie had turned him sooner.

Fletch finally said in a quiet voice, "You reckon I ought to build another coffin, Bess, for the baby?"

I shook my head. "Let him be buried with George. I think Sadie would like that." I remembered Liza and Ruth then. "Where are the girls, Fletch?"

"They're still asleep. They had a bit of a rough night, Bessie, hearing their mama in such pain. I didn't think I'd ever get them to go to sleep. But finally around dawn they dozed off. They were sleeping sound when I left."

"I'll go check on them, make sure they're all right." I turned to go but he caught me by the arm. His eyes bored into mine. "Bess, hearing that last night, I don't think I could stand for you to go through something like that. Maybe it's best if we don't..."

I placed my lips on his. "We won't worry about that now, Fletch." I pressed against him. "I love you," I said before leaving.

The girls were sleeping soundly so I tucked the blanket around them, kissed each on the temple and walked back to my house. I found Miss Ellie in the kitchen starting breakfast. "I'll do that, Miss Ellie," I told her. "You sit and rest."

"I reckon I'm too het up to rest," she said, pursing her lips. She shook her head. "Hate to lose one, it just about kills me ever' time I do."

I patted her shoulder. "I know. I understand that now."

Sadie was still holding her baby boy clutched to her chest. She drew him closer when she saw me.

I sat on the edge of the bed. "Sadie, why don't you let me take him?"

"No, ma'am, you ain't taking my baby." Her eyes were defiant as she edged away from me.

I nodded. "Maybe you should hold him a bit longer." I moved to the rocking chair in the corner and watched her sing to her baby, running her hands over his little body. I knew he would be growing stiff and cold and wondered how long it would take her to finally give him up.

I stopped rocking when Fletcher and Miss Ellie stepped into the room. They had come for the babe and I sensed Sadie wasn't ready to let him go.

She turned to me, tears streaming down her face. "Please, Miss Bessie, don't let them take my baby. They done took my husband, don't let them take my baby."

I stifled a sob. "Miss Ellie just wants to clean him up for you, Sadie," I said in as gentle a voice as I could manage. "She'll let you hold him afterward till you're ready to give him..." I couldn't finish the sentence. I'd been about to say "up" and that sounded so cruel to me.

Sadie clutched him tighter, a stubborn cast to her face. "No, ain't nobody gonna take my baby."

Fletch and Miss Ellie retired to the kitchen and I listened to their low voices as the smell of fried bacon drifted into the room. Sometime later the girls came into the house and tiptoed in the bedroom. I smiled at them and watched as they gingerly approached their mother who showed them their baby brother. When Liza realized he did not live, she sobbed openly but little Ruthie seemed in awe of such a perfect little creature so still and lifeless. Fletch fetched them for breakfast and I shook my head at him when he asked if I wanted to join them. He tilted his head at me and I followed him outside.

"I'm going over to the church," he said, "talk to Preacher Redmon about burying George in the cemetery there."

I nodded. "It's such a lovely graveyard, a good place for George and his baby boy."

Fletch kissed me on the cheek and left, a look of determination on his face.

Finally, around noon, Sadie sat up in bed, the baby in her arms. "I'm ready, Miss Bessie. I want to see him buried with George."

I nodded, went to her and gently took this little sweet boy in my arms. I kissed him on the cheek and told him goodbye and that I was sorry I would never know him, then walked to the barn with him, wishing I could have seen him grow up to be a man like his father had been. I heard a horse coming up the path and looked up to see Fletch riding toward me. He reined in the horse and dismounted, his face hard and angry.

"What happened?" I asked.

"Preacher won't agree to it. Says mayhap we could bury him at the edge of the woods in back of the cemetery but most plots belong to the families around here and there ain't room for George."

"Is it the Red Shirts? Are they afraid of them?"

He shook his head, a look of disgust on his face. "I don't know, Bess, but I raised enough fuss to bring some neighbors running. I let them know what I thought about their unchristian ways."

"We'll bury him here then. He loved this land, Fletcher. It's probably where he would want to rest, don't you think?"

That seemed to appease him. He looked at the bundle in my arms. "Can I have a look at George's boy?"

I pulled back the blanket. "He's beautiful, isn't he?"

Fletch touched the baby's little hands and feet, ran the back of his finger down his soft cheek. "Looks just like his pa, I reckon."

"That he does."

We looked up at the sound of horses thundering our way. Fletch's face got hard. "Put him in the barn with his pa, Bess," he said before stalking off to meet them.

I placed the baby beside George in the coffin, girding myself for a confrontation with the mountaineers, but when I came out saw that several families had gathered around Fletch in the barnyard, all of the men holding shovels. When I joined them, Thorney Dalton stepped forward, hat in hand and said, "We're awful sorry for your loss, Moonfixer. Don't you worry about them Red Shirts. We'll take care of them."

"Thank you, Thorney," I said.

He raised his shovel. "We figured we'd come help Fletch dig the grave, give George and his son a proper burial."

My eyes filled with tears and I couldn't speak. I found myself surrounded by sympathetic women who herded me into the house, their arms filled with food. I looked back at Fletcher and noticed a small group of women entering the barn. I wondered about that until it occurred to me they were going to tend to George and his baby, prepare them for burial, and I thanked God we had such wonderful friends around us.

We buried George and his baby son in a small, flat piece of land near the edge of the forest, a plot Fletcher had set off for our own cemetery. Fletcher had built a fine coffin of cedar, larger that most due to George's size, and I gazed down at George with the baby laying on his chest. The women had done their best with George, dressing him in a nice, dark suit a bit small for him but fitting enough, and cleaning his wounds, although some were such that they could not be hidden. The baby, swaddled in a soft, blue blanket, looked so lifelike, I had to resist picking him up and taking him to Sadie. If not for George's flayed skin, this would have been a beautiful sight. Sadie insisted on seeing her husband but I refused to let her children see him. She became so hysterical, I feared she might pass out, but eventually calmed down enough to nod to Fletcher to close the coffin. I held her hand as we watched the men lower it into the ground and afterward threw yellow snapdragons on top – George's favorite flower. We sang a hymn and Fletcher said a prayer and I walked away, holding Ruth's and Liza's hands to the accompaniment of clods of dirt hitting wood.

When Liza asked me what was going to happen to them, I told her they would stay with us as long as they wanted and Fletcher and I would take care of them and be their family. That seemed to ease her mind a bit but I feared Sadie might not be so accepting of these circumstances and would want to go back to her family in South Carolina. I bit my lip, trying to stall tears. What would I do without these precious girls trailing behind me, asking me to tell them stories and to teach them the alphabet and to gather herbs and wildflowers with?

Sheriff Nanny paid us a visit late that evening, asking me if I could identify the two men on horses. I told him they wore bandanas to hide their faces but their red shirts identified them as such. When he queried if Orson Belle was one of the riders, I had to say no. Both had been too tall to be that little coward. The sheriff left, promising to round up all the Red Shirts he could find and keep them in a jail cell until they revealed who was responsible for George's murder. "I promise you, Moonfixer, whoever did this won't get away with it," he said as he mounted his horse.

But no Red Shirts were to be found, including Orson Belle, which told me he was behind George's murder. At times, I worried that I had caused this, as Sadie once predicted, by humiliating that little man in front of his followers. And when she would look at me, unvoiced accusation in her eyes, I could only tell her how sorry I was and pray this had not come about because of my actions.

The following days passed quickly as I found myself mother to Ruthie and Liza. Sadie spent most of her time huddled in a rocking chair, a blanket clutched tight around her, staring at the mountains surrounding us, leaving her perceived safe harbor only to visit the outhouse or, at my encouragement, to go to bed. It took much effort to get her to eat and only at my insistence that she needed to keep her strength up for her girls. I sensed a hardness in Fletcher, watching each day as he saddled up his horse and rode out, in search of Orson Belle and his Red Shirts, most times accompanied by other mountain men. George's death weighed heavy on his mind and I knew he blamed himself for not taking care of Orson Belle when he tried to hang George. I, too, wrestled with my own guilt, but I fear neither one of us could come to terms with George's death.

Liza and Ruthie followed me around, as silent as shadows, doing what I asked them to, or would lie in bed clutching one another for comfort. I rocked them and sang to them and showed them love and affection but I was not their mother and could never be. Sadie's actions confused them and I could only tell them it was a grieving process for Sadie and she would eventually be their mother as before.

One Sunday, after church, I spied Bull Elliott and Possum Gilliam peeking at me from behind a tree. When Bull caught my eye, he gestured for me to join them. I walked over, glancing around me, wondering what in the world had these two acting so strangely.

When I drew close, Possum yanked me behind the tree with them.

"What in the Sam hill has got you two so het up?" I said, an edge to my voice, as I straightened my sleeve.

Possum darted a quick look around the tree then nodded to Bull, who leaned close to me and spoke in a low voice. "We just wanted to let you know, Miss Bessie, we took care of that matter for you."

"Matter? What matter?"

Bull puffed up. "That matter of a little runt of a Red Shirt runnin' around here stirring up trouble. The one behind what happened to that colored fella you had working for you."

"George? So it was Mr. Belle and—"

"Yep. You ain't supposed to know this but I figure you won't tell nobody that ole Possum's uncle's a member of the KKK. Well, he and his feller Klansmen was all het up about what happened to that colored fella. They figured they'd get blamed for it when they didn't have a thing to do with it and they don't take kindly to visits from the sheriff much less being locked up especially when they done nothing to deserve it. So they set it upon theyselves to find out who was behind it and all it took was a trip to the saloon in Old Fort and a few rounds of drinks with a couple of that runt Orson Belle's friends to find out what happened."

I saw red. "Was he there? Was he involved?"

"Him and about three other men. They followed George till he was by hisself then took him. According to them, they just wanted to scare him enough to make him leave the mountain so tied him behind a horse and drug him a bit, but they'd been drinkin' and things got out of hand, and afore they knew it, ole George was pretty bad hurt. They took him to your farm, hoping you'd be able to do something for his injuries but I reckon he was too far gone."

I clenched my fists. "They did more than drag him, Bull. That poor man had been tortured."

"Well, they won't be hurtin' nobody else, I can assure you of that," Possum said, puffing up his chest. "We took care of things for you."

"What'd you do?"

"Kidnapped that Belle feller and did to him what he did to George."

Alarm stuttered up my spine. "You didn't kill him, did you?"

Bull shook his head. "Nope, just drug him along behind a horse enough to get him all scratched up and tear them fancy clothes he wears."

Possum grinned. "He cried like a little girl and even wet his britches, Miss Bessie."

Before I could stop myself, I said, "I wish he was dead."

Bull nodded. "I'd a killed him if I could, Moonfixer, but he's got that Furnifold Simmons behind him and that man has more power in this state than God hisself. Why, he'd swoop down on us and no tellin' what'd be left of this mountain after he got done with us."

He was right, I knew he was, but that didn't atone for what those Red Shirts did to George. "That Orson Belle's as mean as a striped-eyed snake and about as sneaky, too. Does he know it was you?"

Bull shook his head with a confident look. "We wore bandanas over our faces."

I stared at these two, who at times seemed more child than adult, one tall and burly, the other short and skinny, and was worried for their safety. Everyone on the mountain knew the two of them just by their stature, especially when they were together, which seemed to be more times than not. "Where is he? What happened to him?"

"We blindfolded him, took him down Asheville way, left him out in the woods and told him he better stay off this mountain or the KKK would make sure he never left." Bull snorted. "Little runt was crying like a baby, promising he didn't mean to step on the KKK's toes and we'd never see him again."

"You think he meant it?"

"He better. We're staying alert, Miss Bessie, just in case he tries to sneak back over here."

"What about his friends? Are they still here?"

"Hadn't seen 'em around since they killed your feller. I reckon they heared the Sheriff was after 'em and took off."

"Why didn't you turn Mr. Belle over to Sheriff Nanny?" I asked. "He could have arrested him, along with those other two men, and tried them for murder."

Bull and Possum exchanged glances. Finally Bull said, "That ain't the way it works. Sure enough, the sheriff would arrest him, but like I said, that Furnifold Simmons is a powerful man, and by the time he got through with the sheriff, he'd be out of a job and Orson Belle would be struttin' around here, pretty as you please, knowin' he could do anything he wanted to on this mountain and get by with it. Nope, better to let us handle it. But I'll tell you one thing, he shows his ugly little face around here, that'll be the last anybody'll ever see of him. If Possum and me don't take care of him, Possum's uncle and the KKK will. Don't you fret none. Them Red Shirts don't mess with the KKK. They'll stay away."

I hugged each one, praying they were right, all the while wondering if I had traded one evil for another.

CHAPTER NINETEEN

Early fall 1909

The mill stone grinds slow, but it is always grinding.

While Sadie grieved, Liza and Ruth and I began to spend more time on the mountain, gathering herbs and wild berries. I knew the girls enjoyed these outings and hoped it did them good to spend time away from a mother who was so withdrawn she seemed not to notice the two precious daughters who shared her bereavement over the deaths of their pa and baby brother. As we wandered over the mountain, I would tell them stories my great-grandmother Elisi told me about the Cherokee and it pleased me how much they enjoyed the legends and that they always asked for more.

We set out early one morning to gather ginseng roots to sell, and as we searched under trees, little Ruth let out a squeal of delight. "What'd you find?" I asked, joining her.

She showed me a bracelet made from twisted leather straps, an amethyst glowing golden in the center. "It's beautiful." I brushed caked dirt from between the straps which had darkened to a deep brown from their resting place in the ground.

"Can I have it, Miss Bessie?" she asked, her eyes wide with pleasure.

"First we must ask the Little People for their permission to take it, but if they don't object, I don't see why not."

"Little People," Liza said. "Who are they?"

"Well, it is said the Little People are here to teach lessons to the People about living in harmony with nature and others. They live in rock caves on the side of the mountain and stand only about two feet tall. Some Little People are black, some white and some golden like the Cherokee. Some call them Brownies. They are said to be a most handsome people with hair that almost touches the ground. They love music and spend most of their time dancing, singing and drumming, and are helpful and kind-hearted and work wonders. They have a gentle nature but do not like to be disturbed."

I hid my smile as I noticed Liza studying the side of the mountain, searching for caves of the Little People I was sure.

"What will they do if we don't ask permission?" Ruth said, looking around in hopes of spying one.

"They'll throw stones at us as we go home."

Ruth edged closer to me, clutching my skirt. "What do we say?" she whispered.

"We say, 'Little People, I would like to take this.'" I looked at both girls and smiled. "Are you ready?"

They nodded.

We said the words and waited. When no Little People objected, we continued on our way, both girls darting glances here and there as if in hopes of catching sight of one.

"Tell us more about the Little People, Miss Bessie," Ruth said.

"All right. There are three kinds of Little People; the Laurel People, the Rock People and the Dogwood People. The Laurel People will play tricks and are a mischievous group although they enjoy sharing joy with others. Whereas the Rock People are mean and practice getting even with those who have angered them but they only do this because their space has been invaded. The Dogwood People are a good people who take care of others. But each teaches us a lesson. The Rock People teach us that we must respect other people's limits and boundaries, and that if you are mean to others, it will come back on you. The Laurel People teach us that we must always have joy in our life and share that with others and not take the world too seriously. The Dogwood People teach us a very simple but important lesson, that if you do something for someone, only do it out of the goodness of your heart, not for personal gain or because you feel obligated to."

Both girls were silent for a long moment then Ruth said, "I think I'd like to be a Little People."

"Me, too," Liza said. "I'd like to be one of the Dogwood People 'cause I like helping people, especially Miss Bessie when she's making pies or cobbler."

"I want to be one of the Laurel People," Ruth said in a solemn voice, "cause I like being happy." Her face fell and I knew she was remembering happier times when her father was alive and her world was filled with songs and laughter.

"You both can still be that without being Little People," I said.

The looks they gave me near broke my heart.

When we returned to the cabin, a surprise awaited us: Sadie, sitting in the kitchen looking more pert than I had seen her since George died.

The girls squealed with delight and ran to her, climbing into her lap and hugging her, talking over one another, Liza telling her about the Little People while Ruthie showed her the bracelet, saying, "Look, Mama, it's for you."

"The Little People sent it to make you feel better," Liza chimed in.

Sadie took the gift and hugged her daughters as her eyes lifted to mine. She smiled tremulously and I felt such relief. Mayhap the tea I had been giving her was beginning to take effect. More likely, though, it was the result of her wonderful, caring daughters.

Sadie kissed them and listened as they chattered on about the Little People, but I could tell it took a great deal of effort on her part to not let them see the great sadness that enveloped her.

After they wound down, I said, "Why don't you two take that bracelet down to the creek and wash off all the caked dirt? It's beautiful now but I bet it's a whole sight prettier when it's clean."

They hugged their mother and took off running. Sadie and I looked at one another.

I reached over and took her hand. "What is it, Sadie?"

"I was hoping you could write me a letter, Miss Bess." She glanced away. "I wish I'd taken you up on your offer to teach me how to read and write but it's too late now." Her gaze met mine again. "I reckon you know what I'm wanting."

Tears sprang to my eyes and I blinked hard. "And the reason you're not asking Liza to do it for you."

"It'll only upset her."

I squeezed her hand. "Are you sure, Sadie? You and the girls have a home here with us for as long as you want, the rest of your life if that's what suits you. I love those girls and you, you're all family to me."

"As you and Mr. Fletch are to us, Miss Bess, but we can't live here no more. I lost too much here and with them Red Shirts..."

"They're not around here anymore, Sadie. Some of the mountain men made sure of that and they're going to keep them from coming back, they've promised me that."

She shook her head. "My girls shouldn't never have lost their Daddy like that. I know it weren't your fault but I can't stay here no more. I'm afraid somethin' might happen to my girls and they're all I got left." She placed her hands over her face and began to sob. When she got herself under control, she said, "My brother lives up in Virginia. That's where we was headin' when we come through here. He has his own farm up there and I reckon he'll have room for us. I was hopin' you'd help me write him a letter asking if it was all right for us to come stay with him till we get on our feet."

I got up and fetched pen and paper and wrote the letter for her, trying not to let my tears land on the paper and smear the ink. And when it was done, I told her I'd have Fletch take it to Old Fort and mail it for her.

"I can't thank you for all you done for us," Sadie said, rising to her feet.

I turned my back on her. I could not bear the thought of losing those two beautiful little girls. At times when I despaired I would ever get pregnant, I would console myself that I had Liza and Ruth to mother when I felt the need. Now they would be gone and I would have no child following me around, telling stories Elisi had shared with me. After Sadie left, I stared at the letter, and it occurred to me I could simply throw it in the woodstove and let it burn and mayhap if Sadie didn't receive a reply from her brother, she would reconsider and decide to stay with us. But I sensed this was the way things were supposed to be, they would leave and I could not change it no matter what I did, so that night, I asked Fletcher to take it to Old Fort and then let him hold me as I grieved for two girls I wanted so much to be a part of my life but were not meant to be.

The next weeks passed quickly. I spent as much time as I could with Liza and Ruth, telling them stories, walking with them over the mountainside, letting them help me as I cooked and did chores around the farm. Sadie slowly came back to us and would occasionally join us for a wade in the creek or a picnic on the mountain, and at times I would catch her watching her two daughters, a smile playing around her lips, and knew they would be her salvation and she would be all right.

And one gusty, stormy day, Sheriff Nanny paid us a visit, dropping off a parcel from Old Fort along with a letter from Virginia. When I realized what I held in my hand, I let go as if it were on fire.

Fletcher gave me an odd look, but when he picked it up, his expression changed to one of great sorrow. "I'm so sorry, Bess," he said. I could only nod before leaving him to grieve in private.

I left it to Sadie to tell the girls they were leaving and when they both came running to me, their arms outstretched and tears running down their sweet little faces, all I could do was hold them and tell them how much I loved them and would miss them and hoped they would come back to me one day. I promised Liza and Ruth I would write to them and extracted promises in return to write me back and let me know how they were doing.

Before they left, Fletcher sold the produce from the bountiful garden George had planted and gave the money to Sadie, enough to get them off to a good start if they decided to live on their own. He bought their train tickets to Virginia and they left for Old Fort early on a bright fall morning, the girls crying and holding onto me, pleading with their mother to stay, Sadie trying to be stoic but tears leaking from her eyes, Fletcher watching all this, wringing his hat in his hands, looking agitated and sad.

I waved at the girls as the wagon bounced down the rutted path to the road until I could no longer see them and even then continued to wave, calling my love to them, my face wet with my sadness, and there, off in the distance, I spied a young boy walking toward me. He seemed to be of another world, one hazy and white, but I could see him well enough and I sensed this must be a vision. He was pale and thin and a dark lock of hair fell across his forehead. Why, he looks like Papa must have when he was a boy, I thought. And when he looked up at me and smiled, I knew in my heart this may not be my natural son from my body but a son nonetheless and this boy would be an important part of my life, mayhap the most important part.

Books in the Appalachian Journey series:

Whistling Woman, Appalachian Journey Book 1

In the waning years of the 19th century, Bessie Daniels grows up in the small town of Hot Springs, North Carolina. Secure in the love of her father, resistant to her mother's desire that she be a proper Southern bell, Bessie is determined to forge her own way in life. Or, as her Cherokee great-grandmother, Elisi, puts it, to be a whistling woman.

Life, however, has a few surprises for her. First, there's Papa carrying home a dead man, which seems to invite Death for an extended visit in their home. Shortly before she graduates from Dorland Institute there's another death, this one closer to her heart. Proving yet another of Elisi's sayings, death comes in threes, It strikes yet again, taking someone Bessie has recently learned to appreciate and cherish, leaving her to struggle with a family that's threatening to come apart at the seams.

Even her beloved Papa appears to be turning into another person, someone Bessie disagrees with more often than not, and someone she isn't even sure she can continue to love, much less idolize as she had during her childhood.

And when Papa makes a decision that costs the life of a new friend, the course of Bessie's heart is changed forever.

Moonfixer, Appalachian Journey Book 2

In the dawning years of the 20th century, Bessie Daniels leaves her home town of Hot Springs and travels over the mountains with her husband Fletcher Elliott to live in the Broad River Section of North Carolina.

Bessie and Fletch stay with Fletcher's parents for the first five years of their married life with Bessie teaching in a one-room schoolhouse and Fletcher working at the lumber mill in Old Fort while they save to buy property of their own on Stone Mountain.

In 1906, they purchase 400 acres of the old Zachariah Solomon Plantation which includes a small house with a shack beside it, a branch of Cedar Creek, a row of dilapidated slave cabins…

And ghosts.

Thus begins Bessie's next phase of life where the gift of sight she inherited from her Cherokee ancestors grows stronger, her healing abilities are put to the test, and she encounters a vicious secret society that tries to force her and Fletcher to turn their backs on a family sharecropping and living in one of the cabins.

When Bessie and Fletch refuse to give in to their demands, the group strikes back, bringing pain and suffering to their once serene existence on Stone Mountain.

Bessie travels to the Broad River section of North Carolina with her husband, Fletcher, and assumes her first teaching position at Cedar Grove School while trying to meet the challenges of her new life among the quaint mountain people who call her Moonfixer because she is tall for a woman.

Beloved Woman, Appalachian Journey Book 3

In the second decade of the 20th century, major world events resonate even on secluded Stone Mountain where Bessie Elliott lives with her husband Fletcher. There's a great war, one that takes away many young men, including Bessie's kin, some never to return. Bessie's role of healer intensifies as she treats those with the Spanish flu and tries to keep it from spreading further on her mountain. She defends a young woman who's in the middle of a controversy that threatens to tear her community apart. And she finds herself involved in the suffragette movement as the women of North Carolina fight to gain their rights under the constitution.

Then when one of her family members makes an appalling decision, one that has the potential to damage a child, Bessie impulsively steps in to right the wrong.

Wise Woman, Appalachian Journey Book 4

Traditionally, a Wise Woman is a woman who possesses knowledge, passed down through generations, of time-honored folk medicines. They deal with all kinds of illnesses and medical conditions, often using practical herbal remedies, drawing on plants and the rest of the natural environment, which they know well.

ACKNOWLEDGEMENTS

Once again, we find ourselves with many people to thank for helping us write the second part of our great-aunt Bessie's story, Moonfixer:

First and foremost, we want to thank two talented storytellers: our dad, John Tillery, and his brother, our uncle, Ken Elliott. This book could not have been written without the memories you shared with us about Bessie and Fletch and we are so appreciative.

We especially want to give a huge shout out to the readers of *Whistling Woman*, especially the ones who took the time to email us, like our Facebook page, comment on the Whistling Woman blog, and/or leave us a review. Our amazement at your support and love of the book has been nothing short of...well, amazing! Thank you for letting us know what you thought and for encouraging us to continue Aunt Bessie's story in *Moonfixer*. We know it's been said by countless authors in the past but you are truly the absolute best readers ever!

The people we met and talked with in Old Fort, NC including the docents at the Mountain Gateway Museum and at the Old Fort Train Station and Museum who were very helpful and kindly gave of their time to answer our many questions about the area where Aunt Bessie and Uncle Fletch spent the greater part of their lives. A special thanks to Peggy Silvers, docent of the Mountain Gateway Museum, for sharing interesting history with us regarding secret societies of North Carolina as well as her research on this subject.

Kimberly Maxwell, fellow author, photographer, and cover designer for the beautiful cover. Kimberly used Bessie's actual school bell on the front cover along with a picture of Bessie and Fletcher the day they got married. On the back cover is a painting our dad did of Bessie's and Fletcher's first cabin on Stone Mountain.

Beta readers are an important process in writing a book and we want to give a big thanks to Sherry Cannon, absolutely the best beta reader out there, who helped shape this into a much better read.

There are, again, too many online sites and print books used for research to name them all here but we would like to mention a few:

Find A Grave at http://www.findagrave.com for the lovely pictures of Stone Mountain Missionary Baptist Church and the cemetery where more than a few of the characters in this story are buried;

The North Carolina History site at http://www.learnnc.org/lp/projects/history/ for the informative NC history digital textbook;

Discovery Fit & Health's Herbal Remedies site at http://health.howstuffworks.com/wellness/natural-medicine/herbal-remedies for your Herbal Remedies page;

The Online Etymology Dictionary at http://www.etymonline.com/ for helping us get the words right.

In print, we once again relied on "Long Ago Stories of the Eastern Cherokee" by Lloyd Arneach, "Medicine of the Cherokee" and "The Way of Right Relationship" by J. T. Garrett and Michael Garrett.

All the family members we've met since the release of *Whistling Woman*. We enjoyed getting to know each of you through the miracle of cyber-space and hope one day we can actually meet face-to-face!

Our husbands, Steve French and Mike Hodges, who manage the sometimes crazy world of living with an author with patience and fortitude. Thanks, guys!

And finally, as in *Whistling Woman*, we stayed as true to the family stories and the history in *Moonfixer* as we could but there are times where we took liberties with both. Any and all mistakes and liberties are entirely our own.

ABOUT THE AUTHOR

CC Tillery is the pseudonym for two sisters, both authors who came together to write the story of their great-aunt Bessie in the *Appalachian Journey* series. Tillery is their maiden name and the C's stand for their first initials.

One C is Cyndi Tillery Hodges. Cyndi writers under the pseudonym of Caitlyn Hunter and is author of the *Eternal Shadows* series and *Winds of Fate*, all paranormal romances based on Cherokee legends. She has also written several contemporary romance short stories and a fantasy novella. To find out more about her work, visit her website at http://caitlynhunter.com.

The other C is Christy Tillery French, a multi-published, award-winning author whose books cross several genres. She is the author of *The Bodyguard* series and the *Obsolete* series, as well as several standalone novels. To find out more about her work, visit her website at http://christytilleryfrench.webs.com.

For more information on the *Appalachian Journey* series, the stories and the people it is based on visit, http://whistlingwoman.wordpress.com or find us on Facebook at https://www.facebook.com/appalachianjourney.

.

Made in the USA
Lexington, KY
07 July 2016